Divi

DIVIDING LINES

Victor Sage

CHATTO & WINDUS

THE HOGARTH PRESS
London

Published in 1984 by
Chatto & Windus · The Hogarth Press
40 William IV St, London WC2N 4DF

British Library Cataloguing in Publication Data
Sage, Victor
Dividing lines
I. Title
823'.914[F] PR6069.A3/

ISBN 0–7011–2811 9
ISBN 0–7011–2812 7 Pbk

Typeset by Inforum Ltd, Portsmouth
Printed in Great Britain by
Redwood Burn Ltd
Trowbridge, Wiltshire

TO IAN

CONTENTS

OBSCURITY

The silence in the library was genuine, not imposed. The place was tucked away in a side street and, apart from the lags who snored away wet days like this in the reading room, I was virtually alone. The only sounds were the gentle hiss of the gas fire and the wheezing of the librarian. Strangely, the shelves were full of little black Tauchnitz editions of eighteenth and nineteenth-century novels and I had a theory that he was responsible for them.

Perhaps it was just a visual association: he was very old and tiny, about the size, I imagined, of Toulouse-Lautrec and obviously felt the cold acutely, for he was never, throughout the whole of the summer, without his tight-fitting black overcoat. Whenever the swing door went, he shuffled in his tartan slippers out of a room in the back somewhere and hoisted himself with great difficulty up on to the high stool behind the desk, where he sat, marooned, breathing noisily through his nose, until he could stamp the customers' books.

That nose fascinated me. Olive-green in colour, it sprang directly out of the forehead – but, mysteriously, at a point that seemed to guarantee asymmetry to all the rest of the features – and performed a ruthless arc until it split apart into two coal-black ovals. It was through this dominating organ, that his heavy middle-European accent seemed to issue, and hardly at all from the little mouth, perched below its overhang, that only appeared to serve as hub, for a cartwheel of wrinkles.

My sniff, even the scrape of my feet on the mat, echoed slightly.

'It's raining cats and dogs,' I said aloud, not hearing him stir.

He appeared at the doorway of his den and came a little way into the room as I began to unbutton my mac, but instead of taking up his station at the desk he beckoned to me.

'Come,' he said. 'Dry yourself and get warm for a moment.'

I hung up my mac and bag and followed him across into his little room. There were two chairs in front of the fire, as if he were expecting a visitor. I stood awkwardly.

'Come come,' he said, making a motion with his hands as though he were shooing a goose. 'Sit near the fire, or you won't get the benefit . . . . '

Obediently I sat, rubbing my hands and looking round while he went over to a drawer and began to rummage in it. The little room was triangular – a piece of left-over space in a rather ambitious Victorian design – and it contained what appeared to be a second filing system for the library. The tall window, identical with those in the main hall, was streaked with a yellowish film and steamed up. Pale cords hung down from a pane at the top, which was firmly shut. It gave on to a wall. On the sill, stood a pint bottle of Guinness.

'Will you share it with me?' he said, looking up.

'You've only got one,' I said politely.

'I used to like the ones with screw tops,' he steered the drawer back into position, 'but they're not so easy to come by now.'

He placed the tarnished opener in my hand. I hesitated, again, out of politeness.

'Tell me,' he said, giving me another brief papal shooing as he sank with a long, drawn-out sigh on to the chair opposite, 'why is it you English are so absurdly shy of hospitality?' He took off his spectacles and hooked his finger round a part of his open coat. Very slowly, in minute circles, he started to rub each lens.

With a click the top flew off and the greyish-brown foam welled up; pouring down the side of the bottle, it began to spatter on the floor in front of me. He put back his spectacles and smiled.

'The Englishman never drinks out of the bottle,' he said, 'not like the German. It's as good an index of national character as any.'

Hurriedly, I put it to my lips. He tilted it, I noticed, in a practised hand and drank off about a third.

Steam had begun to rise from my shoes and trousers, and I wondered whether the acrid aroma bothered him, but he took out a small box of Wintermans cigars and, holding it up, cocked his head on one side.

'I don't smoke,' I said, as firmly as I could.

'Wise,' he wheezed, feeling for his matches.

The match flared and illuminated his face. A sentence from the short story I'd once tried to write about him came into my mind, jostling there with the sudden awareness that it was getting dark outside. The failure of that story, I understood now as I watched him get his cigar going, was not a matter of style, as I had thought. It was because it was a fantasy. I simply didn't know anything about him, so my creature had been a mere exotic. Without the resistance provided by facts, there was just a kind of inertia.

Through sheer frequency of contact, we had come to acknowledge one another. At least, I felt so. I felt there was a special familiarity in the way he looked up from the desk and said, 'Exchange, or renewal?' and many a time it had been on the tip of my tongue to ask him a question, but, even as the words formed, I could hear how my voice, shabby, snooping, hollow with ulterior motive, would ring in the empty hall of the library, and I was transported, as I stood in front of him, my eyes glued to the nose that pried to and fro between the covers of my books, back to my tongue-tied schooldays.

Now, as I watched the trail of cigar smoke peeling off continuously in the heat above the fire, I cleared my throat and broke the silence.

'Are you German?'

'Austrian,' I heard him say, as he searched with flapping hand for the bottle under his chair. He sat up.

'And you are trying to become an author, young man.'

The statement, so confidently delivered, seemed uncanny and my face must have registered some surprise because he laughed drily behind the hand that wiped his lips.

'You forget. I have nothing else to do, but observe my few customers.'

He passed over the bottle. I tilted it this time and gulped a mouthful straight down.

'Don't mention that,' I said ruefully. I was suddenly tempted, as I felt the Guinness run down my chin, to confess all. He seemed like a wise, diminutive priest, into whose ears I could deliver safely all my anxieties. Absurdly, I heard an inner voice construct his response, 'Nothing you say, will go beyond these three walls.' But would I be able to confess that he was the subject of, the excuse for, one of my failures?

He stared into the orange bars, the cigar hanging from his lips.

'Obscurity is the fate of most of us,' he said, 'but that's history.'

I didn't understand.

'History is made by the obscure, as much as by the eminent and successful,' he said. He smiled and the way he jerked the bottle in time to his words had the remnant of a toast in it. 'I regard my little victory here over the town council as the making of history as surely as any war.' He laughed. 'To get the county library to take over this building and provide a proper stock of books has been a struggle I have relentlessly pursued. Victory is finally mine. A most obscure victory,' he drank sparingly, 'when one of the conditions of it, is the disappearance of my post.'

'You mean?'

'From the first of next month.'

'But that's *terrible*,' I cried.

'Ah no,' he said, 'I'm old.' He laughed heartily, his shoulders shaking with what seemed a deeply private joke, 'and *not* very prepossessing, eh? It's right for me to go, it's progress.' He held up his finger in mock reproval. 'History consists of these tiny steps by anonymous people. And that's what you authors have the freedom to concern yourselves with. Obscurity is no problem. It is the texture of most people's lives. There's an aphorism for you, "The obscure . . . " ' He paused and searched for a word, ' "The obscure . . . " '

'Can?' I prompted. 'Must?'

'It's gone,' he said, shaking his head and taking another pull at the Guinness.

'But you haven't been here all your life,' I heard myself saying encouragingly.

He stared at me fiercely.

'Young man, you are speaking with someone who has changed the course of history. Without my intervention, the twentieth century wouldn't be what it is . . . '

I laughed.

'That seems a bit of an exaggeration for the County Library . . .'

He waved his hand.

'I'm not talking about that now, I'm talking about something that happened many years ago.'

I was silenced by his tone. I could see that he was moved even by thinking about it. To my slight irritation – my throat was suddenly dry – the bottle in his hand was forgotten, as his eyes roamed unseeingly over the fire and the stacks of files.

The fire hissed on behind the rise and fall of his unfolding sentences. Warm and flushed, the dryness in my throat in its turn forgotten, I listened without effort as he spoke.

'I was born in Vienna. In 1918 my father apprenticed me to the tailor, Hermann Wolff. As you can imagine,' the eyes behind the spectacles gleamed wryly, 'I was a stunted creature, and, though I was bookish, my parents couldn't afford for me to go on at school. I was nine when my father signed the papers, but I looked like an old man, so he added a year or two. Wolff's shop was in the basement of a rambling old place not far from the Berggasse. The top half of the building had been made into a private nursing clinic. Wolff's cellar was always fuggy with the fumes from the oil stove. If it wasn't that, it was the heat from the big old steam press in the corner. The trestles were covered in cuttings and there wasn't much room to move in there.

'For five years, I was remarkably happy. I chattered to him, as I ran back and forth carrying Mr Wolff's materials, his pins, his tuck-markers, needles, pressing irons, and tissue-paper. The hours were long and at night we fell asleep on two greasy truckle beds at either end of the room. All our water was boiled in a blackened kettle placed on top of the oil stove. Not much cause for happiness, you might think, yet I was happy.

'Mr Wolff was no teacher. His attitude was that you learnt things by doing them. He talked in a singsong of instructions, never expecting an answer. For him, I was an extension of his arm to reach his scissors, a kind of two-legged boomerang, that could be trained to pick up at the furthest extension of its flight certain articles. But I was grateful to him. I worked hard and gradually he gave me more and more responsibility.

'One day he went out and left me with a pile of things to press. I set about it with vigour, hoping to finish them before he got back. Sometimes when I worked well he sent me over to the *patisserie* for rum babas. Haste was tricky in pressing: once set in motion the antiquated machine could not be prevented from descending. As I started it, I noticed I had carelessly placed one pair of trousers in the wrong position. If I left them like that, they would be spoilt. The hot press was coming down. I reached in under it to flip back the trouser leg into position, but my sleeve caught. Without thinking, I put my head inside to see what was catching it and the sizzling press hit me just over the bridge of the nose.

'I awoke to find two faces looking at me. Mr Wolff was wringing his hands and pouring forth a stream of self-pity. The other man was Marcus Hajek, the rhinologist from the clinic upstairs. "That's enough, Hermann," said Hajek, "he's not dead at least. I'm doing this as a favour to you, you understand? I'm so crowded out, I have only a small back attic."

'When I came to again, I was lying in a high, barred cot next to a skylight. I fingered my nose. It was covered in plaster and the whole of my face felt numb. Hajek had been forced to saw out part of the bone . . . ' Unconsciously, the hand went up to caress the tip of his nose, ' . . . because my sinuses had been crushed by the accident. But worse, I found that my speech had been impaired so badly, whether by the shock of the accident or the things that had been done to my face I don't know, that I was to all intents and purposes dumb.

'It was about ten days before I could get up and walk, but even then I could do nothing in the way of speaking but grunt . . . ' He broke off, nodding his head musingly. 'I suppose I *was* just like a cretin to look at . . . Anyway, there was a commotion one morning at the door of the little room. I heard them saying, "Easy now" and "Mind the arm" and I wondered for a moment how they were going to get a chair in there, but it was a man, a long-bodied, bearded fellow, in a state of great weakness. Hajek and a nurse were being assisted by two women, one much older than the other, in fur coats. Hajek was still wearing his white overall. The man was fully dressed. Blood had welled through his silver beard and his neat suit and shirt were soaked under the chin with a great bib-like stain. I watched as they settled him on the couch, fussing round him with blankets he didn't want. The two women stood by the door, hesitating. The nurse and Hajek pushed them gently out on to the landing and I heard the woman telling them there was nothing to be done at present. He was out of danger. They should have their lunch, remain as calm as they could, and return in a few hours.

'The nurse came back into the room and went to the couch. She indicated the amber-coloured velvet sash which hung down half-way along its back. The man raised his head and showed her that he understood this was the bell and she went out.

'After twenty minutes he struggled up suddenly into a sitting position. His hand went to the sash. Groaning and striving in vain to mop up the blood that had started to pour out of his mouth, he pulled at it repeatedly. But there was no answer and finally he sank back. Through the bars of my cot, I looked at his face. His cheeks were ashen and the hand, still outstretched, was limp and yellowish. Alarmingly, the stain had started to spread through the blankets . . . '

The librarian paused, and listened.

'Did I hear the door?'

I hadn't heard anything.

But he got up and went to the doorway and listened there, saying that he thought it might be someone come into the library. We both listened.

'It's the rain,' I said. 'Carry on.'

He shuffled back to his chair.

'Finish it,' he said, passing me the bottle, in the bottom of which swilled half an inch of stout.

'One flight down,' he went on, 'I found a nurse. I couldn't talk except in grunts, but I danced up and down in front of her like a monkey, pulling at her skirts and pointing upstairs and eventually she came to see what was the matter. He was in a pitiable state, blood soaking through the blanket, eyes rolling with the effort to stay conscious. She ran for Hajek and after a few minutes of intense activity he managed to stop the bleeding.

'Later on there was a row about how this had happened. I could have told them, but no one thought of asking me. It was discovered in the end, that the sash no longer connected with a bell. When the two women in furs came back, they stood in front of my cot. I grunted at them.

' "Frau Freud," said Hajek to the elder one as they looked down at me, "we don't know how much we owe to this simple good-hearted creature," and I remember her looking down and smiling tearfully.'

I put the Guinness bottle back on the window sill. I was feeling quite unhinged.

'It's a true story,' he insisted. 'Don't look at me like that.'

But I didn't feel sceptical at all, I just felt confused.

'It's the truth,' he repeated, going over to a shelf by the fireside. 'But you won't find my name in here.'

He dragged out a thick tome from under one of the files and put it in my hand. It was the standard edition of the biography of Sigmund Freud by Ernest Jones.

'Your Dr Jones,' he remarked acidly, 'has a somewhat defective sense of the historical process.'

'May I borrow it?'

He nodded, but held up his hand, his ear inclined towards the door. The brass bell on his desk was tinkling.

'Ah, duty *does* call this time.'

He shuffled out. I turned the book over in my hands. It fell open at page four hundred and thirty-nine, where a passage, heavily scored in black pen, instantly caught my eye:

Wife and daughter hurried there to find Freud sitting on a kitchen chair in the outpatient department with blood all over his clothes. The operation had not gone as had been expected, and the loss of blood had been so considerable that it was not advisable for the patient to return home. There was no free room or even a bed in the clinic, but a bed was rigged up in a small room already occupied by a cretinous dwarf who was under treatment. The ward sister sent the two ladies home at lunchtime, when visitors were not allowed, and assured them the patient would be all right. When they returned an hour or so later they learned that he had had an attack of profuse bleeding, and to get help had rung the bell, which was, however, out of order; he himself could neither speak nor call out. The friendly dwarf, however, had rushed for help, and after some difficulty the bleeding was stopped; perhaps his action saved Freud's life.

The phrase 'a cretinous dwarf' and the word 'perhaps' had been triply underlined in red ink and opposite both of them in the margin was a faded exclamation mark.

I looked up. Outside the window, it was completely dark, and the room glowed with warmth.

'Exchange, or renewal?' he was saying to someone through the open door.

DESTROYING ANGEL

Gillian was not coy in the least. She was frank, tall, reasonable, and thirty-six. But she drew the line, it seemed, at nocturnal cohabitation. They were reduced to a series of fleeting struggles, snatched, like fifties teenagers, in cinemas, parks, along canals, and even in the back of her Morris.

Stephen looked up one night from a Hollywood clinch, just in time to see the curtain of the upstairs bedroom window drop.

'Someone was watching,' he said, 'I saw them.'

'Yes,' said Gillian, looking round for her handbag, 'I'd better go in.'

'Was that your daughter?'

'I'd better go,' said Gillian, 'I . . . I'll see you.'

'Yes, but *when*?'

'Oh, I don't know . . . Soon . . . Call me at work tomorrow evening.'

'Why can't I ever call you *here*?'

'Better at work,' she threw back over her shoulder, as she strode, waving, round the front of the car.

'Look,' said Stephen when he called her, 'do you have another man?'

Gillian burst out laughing.

'I'm serious . . . I mean, are you avoiding me?'

'Of course not.'

'Do you *want* to make love with me?'

'What do you think we were doing at the Observatory the other night?'

'In a *bed*?'

'Look,' said Gillian, 'I can't talk now. Someone's come into the ward. I'll ring you back, OK?'

When they met, Stephen said they *must talk*. Gillian insisted on driving along by the side of the tennis courts. There was a little gully, she said, with guaranteed privacy. They parked in the

car-park and walked, swinging their hands, to the wire netting.
They gazed at the empty space, the sagging nets.

Gillian said she thought it was just the place to begin a divorce, or
to part. But Stephen was boiling up to his semi-rehearsed speech:
They had been going out together now for several weeks and they
hadn't even seen each other with their clothes off. He looked
sidelong, one of his most winning poses. He didn't understand.
She didn't seem to resist him. So why did they have to resort to all
these absurd, *acrobatic* encounters? Did she think it was more
romantic that way?

Gillian was hysterical. She clutched the wire netting like a
prisoner. She rattled it in mock desperation.

He went on: he didn't understand. They had a lot to give each
other. It was obvious. They both wanted it. Why *couldn't* they
sleep together?

Gillian pealed with laughter:

'You'll be telling me I'm not like other girls next!'

'You're not.'

'And you're not like other *men*!' she shrieked.

On the far court, one of the players turned round.

'I thought you liked me,' said Stephen, aggrieved.

'Oh I *do*,' breathed Gillian, her face a mixture of satire and
anxiety.

She lifted up her skirt.

'Look what I've got on for you.'

He looked down at the lean brown thighs that ended in a pert vee
of mauve crepe.

But Stephen was confused. All this frank behaviour, why not
put it on a regular footing? Why shouldn't he come home with her?

For answer, Gillian sank into the grass and put her arms round
his knees.

'Please,' she murmured.

'No,' said Stephen, 'we don't *need* to do it like this. It's undigni-
fied. Baring your bottom at our age. What the hell's going to
happen when the winter comes?'

'Come on,' said Gillian, nudging him, 'you're all of twenty-
eight. Remember your Elvis.'

She sang, contralto, lifting her throat:

> Let the stars fade and fall
> And I won't care at all
> As long as I have . . . yoooooooo.

Far off, a tense rally came to a halt as the players searched the dusk for the noise.

Gillian's lips were parted, her eyes closed.

'Why can't I meet her?' said Stephen. 'Let's go back tonight, please?'

But she was swinging away from him over the grass.

'What's the matter? I'm good with kids.'

As he ran along by her side, he saw the tears in her eyes.

'You fucking silly bastard,' she cried, as they reached the car, 'leave me alone.'

'Isn't it enough,' she shouted, afterwards. 'Isn't it enough for you?' ripping the tyres round on the shales of the car-park.

The girl holding the bloody carving knife stared at him briefly, and began backing away, open-mouthed, into the dimness of the hall.

'It walks. It talks,' he thought he heard her say.

Flattening herself against the wall in order to get by, Gillian came to the door.

'Oh it's you.'

'What?'

'Well,' said Gillian, glancing behind her, 'I didn't expect you after the other night.'

'Was that Tanya?'

'Yes.'

'She didn't look too bad,' said Stephen brightly. 'Do we have to talk out here on the doorstep?'

'No of course not,' said Gillian. 'Now that you've come.'

He followed her into the dark hall.

'Have a sit in here,' said Gillian. She pointed vaguely to a door. 'I'll make some tea.'

But within a moment, she came back, the strain showing on her features.

'Tanya's going to make it.'

'What's the matter?'

'Nothing,' said Gillian. 'In here.'

She showed him into the front room. In the middle of the carpet, on a square of newspaper, lay a mound of fur and entrails.

They looked at it.

'What's that?' said Stephen.

'Oh it's . . . nothing,' said Gillian. 'Just something of Tanya's. I'll just get the thing and wipe it up.'

The door flew open and banged against the wall.

'Stay where you are,' said a voice. 'I'm coming in.'

'Tanya, this is Mr Wallis,' said Gillian.

Stephen smiled, holding out his hand.

'Hello Tanya,' he said warmly.

He looked down in time to see that Tanya's stumpy fingers were covered in bloodstains. A sticky red hand slid into his and Tanya smiled into his eyes with her mouth.

'Ah yam so gla to meet you Meesterr Wallisss,' she said, 'beecoss effery fren' of Gillian, hee ees a fren' of min-ah.'

Stephen tried to remove his hand, but she was still smiling and pumping the red hand up and down in his.

'Sugar?' said Tanya, in quite another voice.

'Two please,' said Stephen, negotiating the pile on the carpet and sitting down again.

'Two for *you* . . . and two for *me* . . . and, for Gillian, her usual,' she laughed and threw back her head, 'sixteen and a half. Oh, what a funny little Mummy she is. She has *such* a sweet licker tussypeg. Don't you, Mum?'

'Tanya, please,' said Gillian.

'Now Gilliewillie,' said Tanya, handing her a cup in which a browning Matterhorn of sugar protruded above the liquid, 'dwinkie-winkie . . . '

Stephen leant across to Gillian.

'How's work?' he asked, 'I've not been able to get hold of you there. I rang the ward, but they said they didn't know where you were.'

'Gillian hasn't been feeling very well lately,' Tanya broke in, looking down her nose like a headmistress. 'You see Mr Wallis she caught rather a cold on the tennis courts the other night.'

Her mouth opened and her tongue lolled out as she leaned over and patted Gillian's knee.

'Been going out rather a lot lately,' she fruited, '*haven't* we?'

'Stop it in front of Mr Wallis,' said Gillian.

'What on earth shall we do when he's gone, darling?'

'I said stop it.'

'Gillian and I have been chatting recently,' said Tanya, 'and we've decided, you see, that it might be better for her to go back on nights for a while.'

Gillian stood up.

'If you don't get this mess off the floor in two seconds flat,' she thundered, 'there's going to be trouble.'

Tanya picked up the carving knife from the teatray.

'Huh,' she said. 'You fuckin' try anythin' . . . '

'What *is* that anyway?' asked Stephen, pointing.

'If you must know,' said Tanya, 'it's Roadrunner our cat. We found him in the alley.'

She dropped on one knee and began wrapping it up in another sheet of newspaper.

'And I suspect the old bag across the road's poisoned him. So I've dissected him. And I'm taking him into biology on Monday.'

She walked to the door, the blood beginning to drip through the newspaper on to the carpet.

'I shall continue my work in the bathroom. Will someone please help me with the door.'

Stephen shut the door after her.

'She really needs getting a grip of,' he said.

'Why did you have to come?'

'I was worried about you, for God's sake. I rang and rang . . . '

'I am perfectly all right. I just need to be left alone.'

'You need *help*.'

Instantly, through the ceiling, came a parodic rendition of Max Bygraves:

> You need *hainds*
> To howuld you . . .

Gillian sighed. 'I wish those workmen hadn't made that hole when they put the new pipes in. She can hear every word.'

The singing stopped. Steps ran across the floor and they heard her coming down the stairs, one step at a time. A yell of horror, cut off by sobbing, sounded in the hall.

Slowly the door opened.

'What is it?' said Gillian in a monotone, holding out her arms.

The face was pinched and blotched with a misery so absolute that her features gave only a rough estimate of it. A heavy lowing sound leaked through her corrugated lips.

They swayed together in the centre of the room, while Gillian patted her back and stroked her hair.

'What is it, darling, have you hurt yourself?'

Tanya shook her head from side to side and put her thumb in her mouth.

'Well what are you making all this silly noise for?'

'Not filly,' said Tanya, through her thumb.

'I can't hear you.'

Tanya took out her thumb.

'It's not silly,' she pronounced, 'I can't find any clean knickers for tomorrow. It's all your fault . . . You've got to go to the laundrette now.'

'I'm tired, darling,' said Gillian, 'I've been at work all day.'

'Nothing's ever any good here,' shouted Tanya, striking the chair arm with her bunched fist. 'How do you expect me to do my homework for Monday, when there aren't any clean clothes for me to wear?'

'If the worst comes to the worst,' said Gillian, 'you can always borrow a pair of mine.'

Tanya smiled broadly and drew in her breath.

'Can I? Oh good.'

She turned away from Gillian's embrace, but her face clouded over again.

'Ohhh . . . but there's something else.'

'What now?'

'I can't find my trom*bone*, Mum . . . I can't find it *anywhere*.'

'Have you left it at school again for anyone to pinch, you careless little monkey? I paid one hundred and twenty pounds for that thing!'

'Mum I just don't know, I don't remember.'

'Well, think!' yelled Gillian.

'I can't!' she wailed, bursting into tears.

'I'm not buying you another one. So you'd better try!'

'I can't . . . really I can't.'

'I bet it's upstairs,' said Gillian suddenly.

Tanya's expression softened.

'It's not,' she said.

But she was laughing openly, her shoulders shaking, her head moving rhythmically from side to side.

'Honest, Mum.'

'It's in your room,' said Gillian. 'If I have to come up there, I shall be *very cross*.'

'Oh . . . all right,' said Tanya, coolly drifting out.

They came back from the pub at closing time to find Tanya in her Victorian nightdress, standing arms akimbo halfway up the stairs.

'Where d'you think you've been?'

'Out,' said Gillian defiantly.

'You've been to that pub haven't you?'

'What's it to you,' said Gillian giggling.

Tanya's face caved in.

'You don't care about me!' she said, plumping down on the stairs and covering her face with her hands. 'You don't care at all, do you?'

Gillian grinned callously.

'You don't,' said Tanya. 'Anyone could come in here . . . '

'Wouldn't stand much of a chance with you,' said Gillian thickly. 'Would he, dear?'

Stephen made a masterful lunge up the stairs.

'What are you on about,' he grabbed her round the waist. 'You cheeky little monkey.'

Tanya screamed and caught him the lightest of slaps on the cheek, as he hoisted her up on his shoulder.

'Time you were in bed, young lady,' he said.

Tanya reclined on his shoulder thumb in mouth.

'Pooh,' she said, 'you smell.'

'That's enough of that,' said Stephen firmly, mounting the stairs. Tanya was looking over his shoulder at Gillian. She took her thumb out again.

'You both smell,' she said and then, as an afterthought, 'and Mum's been boozing the money away at that pub.'

Stephen turned round.

'Which is her room?'

Gillian was leaning ironically, hands in the pockets of her fur coat, against the wall.

'Straight ahead.'

'It's my money,' wailed Tanya, 'and you've been spending it at that pub.'

Gillian almost ran to the bottom of the stairs.

'What do you mean, your money?'

'My Child Benefit Allowance,' said Tanya, pushing out her pug jaw. 'You just spent it, haven't you? You hadn't got any other money in your purse.'

Gillian clapped her hand laughingly over her mouth.

'My God,' she said, 'so I have.'

The pug jaw began to buckle.

'It's not fair,' said Tanya, 'I wanted to buy a new blouse with it tomorrow.'

Gillian came up the stairs after them.

'Darling, you'll get the money. It's just a question of liquidity, that's all.'

'What's that supposed to mean? I *want* it. You said you'd give it me every week. You *said* . . . '

Stephen pushed open the door of Tanya's room. It was howling with heavy rock music. He dumped her on the bed and switched off the tape.

'No!' screeched Tanya, 'I have to have it *on*!'

'What?'

Gillian explained from behind that Tanya always went to sleep every night with a tape of the Rolling Stones or her radio on.

'Better let me,' she said, brushing past him into the litter of sheet music and dirty underwear.

'Darling, I work . . .' Stephen heard her say as she closed the door.

He was woken by Gillian's kiss. The light from the curtains was so dim, he was looking up at her face as if through water.

'Here's some tea, my love,' she said.

As he took the cup, fragments of the evening before came back: their nakedness, their blind greedy wanderings while Tanya's music had thumped away in the next room.

'Work?'

She screwed up her face.

'Mmm, 'fraid so.'

'What's happening with . . .?' he asked anxiously.

Gillian laughed, and kissed him again.

'It's all right. I'm not leaving you alone with her. She's going to Mrs Coley.'

Stephen sighed and stretched.

'You make me feel lazy,' he purred.

'You are,' murmured Gillian, bending to kiss him again.

The door flew open and Tanya marched to the wardrobe mirror.

'Mum,' she said, looking sideways at herself, 'we're going to be late.'

'Wish you were in here with me,' said Stephen under his breath.

'Mmm . . .' said Gillian, drawing away.

'What's that funny smell,' said Tanya, pirouetting.

'Smell?' said Stephen. Gillian stood up.

'We must go,' she said.

Tanya came to the bottom of the bed.

'Yuck,' she said, 'it smells of *bum* in here!'

'Bye-bye,' said Gillian, bending over him again.

'Mum!' wailed Tanya like an air-raid siren, 'pleeeeese. Lets-go-I'm-go-ing-to-be-laaaaate.'

'Say goodbye to Stephen,' said Gillian.

But the door had closed.

Stephen lay for some time after they had gone, toying with a stiff cock, dreaming over the nooks and crannies of Gillian's body.

When he woke again, it was eleven-thirty. He sat up, a busy man.

He swung over the side of the bed, yawning, and planted both feet on the floor. Between them, something glowed whitely. He picked it up. It was a fragment of eggshell. Stephen made a mental note to mock Gillian about having breakfast in bed, and drew on his underpants.

Feeling a shock of wetness under his scrotum, he let down the underpants and examined himself. From his balls dripped a glutinous mess of amber and, in the crotch of the underpants, accusingly, lay the corresponding pool of transparent slime.

He came across Tanya on the landing, aimlessly dragging round her velvet toad, thumb in mouth.

'For God's sake, what d'you think you're doing?'

She looked coldly at him.

'You know what I mean: these!'

He waved the egg-stained underwear.

'Thunno,' said Tanya through her thumb.

Stephen looked at the cold face, turned up in its pug-like expression, and felt sick. She leaned against the bathroom door and swung the toad casually by its arm.

Stephen dropped on one knee.

'You know what I'm talking about,' he said, 'you little creep. You did this, didn't you?'

Tanya shook her head.

'Who else could have done it?'

She trailed away into her bedroom, pulling the toad after her.

'Come here,' said Stephen helplessly.

Tanya slammed the door.

Stephen pushed it open.

Above the bed on which she lay, face down, was a picture of Gillian, in her nurse's cape. Next to that was a newspaper photograph of an Indian woman sitting crosslegged and holding, against the flesh of her bare forearm, a striking cobra. He read the caption:

SNAKES ALIVE! A cobra bites an Indian woman who wants to get high on its poison, a substitute for heroin. The woman first makes the cobra use up most of its venom by biting something then gets her kicks.

'Go away,' said Tanya into the sheets.

Stephen sat on the bed.

'Get off my bed.'

'Don't you like me?' he asked.

Tanya shook her head from side to side.

'D'you hate me?'

The head wagged up and down.

'Why, Tanya?'

'Go away,' said the muffled voice.

'Is it because of your Mum?' said Stephen.

Tanya was silent.

'Listen, Tanya. There's no need to be jealous of me, you know. I'm not going to take your Mum away from you.'

Tanya was still.

'Tanya, please, look at me.'

He reached down to turn her over, catching her on either side of the waist. But Tanya's hand flailed backwards and hit him under the eye.

'Get *off*,' she said, squirming away.

His eye was watering and Stephen suddenly let go. He stood up and sighed falsely, aware of an erection like a hatrack in his trousers. Hastily, he put his hands in his pockets. Money jingled.

Tanya's eye opened.

Stephen took out fifty pence and sighed again.

'Of course, if you don't want this . . . '

Tanya turned slowly, her tartan skirt riding up her thigh. The coin lay in his palm.

'One condition,' he said.

'Wha?'

'You don't say anything to Gillian about this and you don't ever do it again.'

Tanya rolled back, closed her eyes and put her thumb in. He could see the sunlight glinting in the blonde hairs behind her knees.

'Thass *thoo* fings,' she said drowsily, 'and thoo fings is worf *thwice* as much.'

❋

When pressed in a whisper, Gillian admitted a similar ache, but 'Ssssh . . . I think she's listening,' terminated any conversation. There were simply no arrangements to be made. Gillian went back to composing and recomposing her long brown legs, the black sunglasses closing off all expression from her face. Stephen rolled over and goggled at the same blazing page of *Voyage of the Beagle*. Tanya sat a few feet away, letting the sand trickle through her fingers, eyeing and sighing.

'Mum, I'm bored. What did we have to come here for?'

'To get brown dear.'

'It's a mouldy seaside. There's nothing to do, Mum.'

Gillian raised a lens.

'Go for a walk.'

'I don't want to by myself.'

'Go in the sea,' said Gillian, 'go *some*where, love.'

'I can't swim.'

Stephen was stroking Gillian's arm.

Tanya tossed back her ropes of yellow hair and stood up.

'All right,' she said, 'I *am* going for a walk.'

'Little Madam,' said Gillian as they watched her red swimsuit recede to a blur along the tideline.

'We could slip back to the hotel,' said Stephen. He began to kiss her toasting belly.

'You've got sand in my oil,' said Gillian. 'No,' she sighed, 'let's just . . . '

And the sporadic noise of the French family next door, the distant shouts of '*VoilassieursDames, les burna glassa* . . .' and the wash wash of the sea overtook the ache and the dazzle.

'My God,' said Gillian sitting bolt upright. 'Where is she?'

For a mile Stephen stumbled behind her as she ploughed through sandcastles and late lunch parties, wringing her hands and turning back to him to say, 'Oh my God, where can she be?'

The beach was crowded, now that the midday sun had gone down. There were blonde girls in red swimsuits everywhere, it seemed, screaming in the water or riding on the shoulders of their boyfriends.

'I can't stand it,' said Gillian. 'What are we going to do?'

'She'll turn up,' said Stephen. 'She can't have gone far.'

'Two hours. It's two hours.'

'Don't worry.'

'But she can't *swim*, the little bitch!'

At last they decided that Tanya couldn't possibly have come as far as they had, and turned back. Stephen tried to ask a tea lady in a booth whether she'd seen a girl in a red swimsuit, but after a word or two she shrugged and turned back to her other customers.

'Fat lot you can speak,' said Gillian looking round for a policeman.

On the way back to their spot, they had to thread their way through the teeming families, all packing away their windbreaks and parasols. They were exhausted, snapping at one another as they plunged on through the leaden sand.

'This is ridiculous,' Stephen heard himself say.

But Gillian was running like the wind.

When he caught up, she was down on her knees in the sand. Tanya's expressionless face appeared over her shoulder as Gillian embraced her tightly and, for a long moment, she stared unwaveringly at Stephen. Then her eyes closed and a red stub pushed and pushed until it hung, obscenely long, from the middle of her sneer.

The Morris rolled to a halt at the edge of the cornfield. Stephen raised his head from the map and looked across at Gillian.

'Oh for God's sake, Tanya love,' said Gillian.

'Now let's see . . . we're here . . .' He leant across to show Gillian, but the breathing from the back-seat was thick and fast like a worn-out concertina.

'Tanya,' said Gillian, 'you're getting hysterical.'

Tanya screamed.

'Something touched me! A spider!'

'. . . and the château is about . . . here.'

'There's a spider in this car.'

'Now if we take this little road here . . . '

'Oh, that's quite enough,' said Gillian swinging round.

Stephen stared at the corn.

'Oriental and immortal wheat,' he said. 'Where does that come from?'

'It's not wheat,' said Tanya, 'is it, Mum?'

'It's fucking wheat,' said Stephen.

'It's fucking not,' said Tanya.

'Tanya, watch your language,' said Gillian. Her hands tightened on the wheel as she pulled across the road.

'I like that,' said Tanya. 'Huh, *he* can swear, why can't I? Tell *him* off!'

'Reminds me of Lincolnshire this,' said Stephen.

'Yes,' said Gillian, looking in the mirror. 'Tanya, what's the matter now?'

Stephen turned round. The moist eyes were ringed with purple. Half triumphant, Tanya sniffed.

'Wish we'd never come,' she said, looking out of the window. She brightened, 'Mum?'

'Darling, I'm trying to drive.'

'I want "Saturday Night Fever" on,' said Tanya, blowing her nose and examining the contents of her handkerchief.

'Oh, we don't want that racket on,' said Stephen to Gillian, 'do we?'

'Well I'm going to have it,' said Tanya. 'So there.'

'No,' said Stephen.

'Huh, *you* can't stop me,' said Tanya, rummaging in her plastic carrier for the cassette.

'We're not having it on,' said Stephen. He slipped his arm over the back of the seat and prised it out of her fingers.

'Who d'you think you are,' said Tanya furiously struggling with him, 'I'll *kill* you, you fucking horrible . . . '

'Right!' shouted Gillian, 'Tanya, put those tapes away this minute!'

'Oh *Mum*, that's not fair . . . just because *I* wanted it on . . . you have to do what *he* says all the time, don't you?'

In the silence which followed, Tanya sat with a hand under each armpit. Out of the corner of his eye, Stephen saw the right hand steal out from under the fall of coarse hair, fingers tilting upright, on its furtive ascent to the nose. Three repelled but reassuring sniffs, and it vanished.

'Do we have to go and see this château thing?' she said in a high whine.

'Yes,' said Gillian, too quickly.

'Why?' said Tanya.

'Because I want to,' said Gillian. 'That's why.'

'I don't,' said Tanya.

'We're going to do something that *I* want to do for a change,' said Gillian boldly. 'Besides,' she added, 'it won't take long.'

'It will . . . it'll take ages,' she wailed. 'Oh, why did we have to come off the N20? We'll never get home by Tuesday now.'

'We're supposed to be on holiday,' said Gillian desperately.

'What on earth do you want to get home by Tuesday for?' asked Stephen.

'Never you mind,' said Tanya. 'It's none of *your* business.'

'You don't have any school,' he insisted.

'If you must know,' said Tanya, 'I want to go and see my Father.'

'Where do we go here?' Gillian asked.

'Take the left,' said Stephen. 'No, the left . . . '

'I'm sorry,' said Gillian. In the field, a face the colour of mahogany looked up as she ground the gears and sent the car howling back towards the junction.

'I did say,' Stephen muttered.

'That man thinks you're mad,' said Tanya.

'How far is it now, love?' said Gillian, looking over to Stephen.

'Ugh,' said Tanya, 'something smells funny in this car.'

Automatically, in ragged triplets, they sniffed, Tanya leading.

'Nothing smells,' said Stephen. 'For Christ's sake!'

'I think I'll wash my hair tonight,' said Tanya.

'God, I hope there's a bar in this village,' said Stephen.

'Anyway,' said Tanya, renewing the attack, 'what's *at* this château, Mum, what's the point of going there, when it's only old furniture and stuff.'

'Look in the book,' said Gillian to Stephen.

'Ah, here we are,' Stephen bent back the cover of the guide book, 'the Château of Talcy is thirty-two kilometres from the

N20,' he began to read. 'Situated in the village of Talcy, a sixteenth-century château of considerable importance. It was here that a meeting took place between the Protestant and Catholic parties of France in 1597. Some eighteenth-century restoration.'

'Mmm,' said Gillian, 'sounds interesting.'

'You only said that because *he's* here,' said Tanya musingly. 'Didn't you, Mum?'

'What do you mean?' said Stephen, whipping round.

Tanya cocked her head and smiled.

'She's only pretending to be interested, because you are. Aren't you, Mum?'

'Aren't we nearly there?' said Gillian.

'Yes,' said Stephen, 'judging by the map, we should be able to see it when we get round the next corner.'

'Mum, can I have the Rolling Stones on?' said Tanya.

'No,' said Gillian. 'Oh, isn't it pretty!'

'Oh,' said Tanya, 'isn't it *pwetty*!'

'Don't be so unpleasant, Tanya,' said Gillian.

'Honestly Mum,' said Tanya, throwing her arms round Gillian's neck, 'if you could just *hear* what you sound like sometimes.'

'Ohhh,' said Gillian, as Stephen entered her from behind. 'Oh, that's lovely.'

It was. It was indescribably what the doctor ordered. It was what both of them had needed for two weeks of short-tempered abstinence.

When the door creaked open, Gillian only just managed to reach behind and throw up the sheet.

'What you doin' Mum?' said Tanya, standing by the side of the bed.

'Don't you ever knock?' said Gillian through her teeth.

'What are you *doing*?' said Tanya, her eyes flickering over their strange piggyback. 'Why's it so hot in here?'

Stephen felt himself shrinking. After a few more seconds of Tanya's scrutiny, he slipped out of Gillian with an almost perceptible 'plop'.

Tanya's eyes jumped.

'What was that?' she said.

'What was what?' said Stephen with a groan, as he collapsed on the pillow.

'That funny noise. Did you just let off?'

Gillian subsided too with a weary sigh.

'Don't be disgusting, Tanya.'

'Mmm,' said Tanya, 'you've got a big spot on your nose.'

'Oh,' said Gillian. 'Oh how *erotic*!'

'What's that mean?'

'Never mind,' said Gillian.

'Pooh, you have let off. There's a funny smell in here.'

'Oh, for God's sake, Tanya,' shouted Gillian, 'will you go away!' Then, soothingly, she murmured, 'I'm just getting up now darling.'

Tanya's face was frozen. She banged her knees against the side of the bed.

'It's half past twelve,' she said, 'and I want to go to town.'

'I'm not stopping you,' said Gillian.

Simultaneously, two tears grew in Tanya's eyes, making them look to Stephen like blobs of frogspawn. The shoulders shook, the chin wrinkled, the lips bubbled with one dry sob.

'What's the matter?' said Gillian.

'You said you'd come with me to get that skirt. I can't choose it by myself, you know that!'

'I forgot,' said Gillian, half turning to Stephen, 'I did promise her.'

'Oh for God's sake,' said Stephen to the ceiling.

Gillian lifted back the sheet and swung her legs over.

'*Great!*' said Tanya, drawing in her breath in ecstasy, the tears running down into her smile.

'Oh, you do *want* to come, don't you, Mum?' she said, 'I don't want you to come if you don't want to.'

She skipped to the door as Gillian swayed upright.

'It's not a very big spot,' she said eagerly. 'In fact, Mum, I can hardly see it at all from here.'

Gillian pouted and fell back into Stephen's arms.

'Bye love, see you later.'

'Bye.'

'Oh, don't be like that!'

'I'm not,' said Stephen.

'Don't *you* start making me feel guilty for God's sake.'

'Bye now,' Tanya said sweetly to Stephen. 'Have a nice day!'

Gillian held the box, while Stephen held the book. From time to time, Tanya dashed off into the bracken on either side of the track. She reappeared some yards further up, beckoning.

'Look. Look at these.'

They gazed at the pale yellow caps, stacked like village rooftops on the stump of beech.

'Let me guess,' said Stephen, leafing through the book. 'Two-toned pholiota.'

Tanya shook her head. 'Cheat. Anyway you're wrong. They're Honey Fungus.'

'How can you tell?'

Tanya knelt and prised back a piece of bark.

'See?'

They looked at the tiny, bootlace-shaped rhizomorphs.

'Quite the expert, aren't we,' said Gillian archly.

'It's only the book, you know,' said Stephen.

'Oh Mummy,' cried Tanya, rushing up against Gillian. 'Oh, my Mummy.'

'Careful,' said Gillian, 'you'll upset the box.'

Tanya sucked in air through her front teeth. Her eyes darted.

'I'll never leave my Mummy,' she said through gritted teeth.

Gillian laughed over at Stephen.

'Everyone has to some day,' he said.

'Not me,' said Tanya.

'Even you,' said Stephen.

'That's not right,' said Tanya, hanging heavily on the sleeve of Gillian's coat. 'He's not right, is he?'

Gillian looked down.

'Don't be silly,' she said sharply. 'Act your age, you silly girl.'

'I am,' said Tanya putting in her thumb.

'And do stop that,' said Gillian, shaking free her sleeve.

The pines dripped condensing mist as they walked in silence down the track, Tanya dragging and shuffling through the waist-high ferns.

'Oh look,' she cried, 'look at these.'

'Real fairy toadstools,' said Gillian.

'Fly agaric,' said Stephen. 'Otherwise known as . . . hang on . . .'

'Wow,' breathed Tanya, kneeling in the bracken, 'aren't they *red*.'

She stretched out her hand.

'Don't touch, darling,' said Gillian automatically. 'They're not nice.'

'D'you know what they do with these in Lapland?' said Stephen. 'They feed them to their deer and then . . .'

'Drink the deer's wee,' said Tanya.

'How do you know?' said Gillian.

'It's in the book,' said Stephen.

'What on earth for? I thought they were poisonous.'

'Oh *Mum*,' said Tanya. 'Don't you know anything. To get high of course.'

They turned and wandered off, leaving Tanya kneeling in front of the toadstools.

'Let's have a look,' said Stephen, peering into the box. 'My God, we've some lovely ones in there.'

'Must keep these Lawyers Wigs separate,' said Gillian, 'and marinade them, like we did when I was a child.'

'Stephen Stephen,' shouted Tanya, 'let me have the book for a minute please.'

'What for?' shouted Stephen without turning round. 'What have you found?'

He felt the book torn from his hands.

'If I knew, silly,' said Tanya by his elbow, 'I wouldn't be asking would I?'

They walked on, the pine twigs going off like damp squibs under their feet.

'You are clever,' said Gillian, leaning her head on his shoulder. 'That book was such a good idea for a present.'

'She must have read it fifty times already,' said Stephen. 'She won't let anyone else get at it.'

'I am grateful to you,' said Gillian, 'for persevering with her.'

'Well, I can't really believe the way she's behaving.'

'Maybe she's going to be a botanist, and you've set her on the track.'

'A mycologist.'

'Oh,' said Gillian, clapping her hand over her mouth. 'Look over there.'

'Stinkhorns,' said Stephen.

'They're just like . . . '

'Got it in one. *Phallus impudicus*.'

'I shall have to read this wretched book,' said Gillian.

They paused. In the middle of the clearing, six inches high, stood the curved white stems, their greenish, acorn-shaped tops coated in flies.

'Wait for me,' came Tanya's wail from somewhere down the track.

Stephen turned to Gillian and slipped the tip of his wet tongue inside her opening mouth. They stood nuzzling for a moment in the centre of the track, vaguely aware, out of the corner of their eyes, of the blur of Tanya's new blue parka.

When they looked round she was staring at them, the book hanging limply from one hand. In the fingers of the other a button mushroom dangled by its short stem.

'Come on, darling,' said Gillian.

'What have you got there?' said Stephen.

Tanya was silent. They ran to her.

'What's the matter?' said Gillian.

Stephen tried to pick the mushroom out of her hand, but she held it tightly.

'No. It's mine. I found it.'

'I don't care,' said Stephen, gathering up the box, 'it'll be a great stew without *yours*.'

'Wanna go home,' said Tanya decisively.

Through the bars at the bottom of the bed, he watched Gillian lift up her nightdress and pull on her striped pants.

'Dressing is sexier than undressing,' he said dreamily. 'They ought to have clubs where people dress.'

'Are you going to be all right today?' said Gillian, looking in the mirror.

'Of course.'

'I shall be home at three.'

The bangs on the bedroom door came solemnly, with long intervals between.

'I told you to knock,' said Gillian opening it, 'not to bash the door in.'

Tanya marched in, the book under her arm, and sat on the bed.

Gillian put her hand on Stephen's forehead.

'Poor lamb. You're so hot. Still feeling queasy?'

'A bit better thanks.'

Tanya lay across the bed humming.

'I've made you some broth out of the remains of that chicken,' said Gillian. 'Make sure she gives you some.'

'D'you hear me?'

Tanya nodded vigorously.

Gillian came round the bed.

'I must rush now, darling . . . '

'Tra Mum,' said Tanya, intervening, and tendered upside down her rosebud kiss.

'You look after Stephen,' said Gillian. 'I'm relying on you.'

Tanya rolled towards him until she lay across his chest.

'I said look after him, not suffocate him.'

After she had gone, Tanya lay across the bed, still humming, her thumb in her mouth, her legs wide open. Her left hand strayed towards the hem of her skirt. The book lay closed at the bottom of the bed, forgotten.

'D'you want to come inside?' said Stephen.

'Wha?'

'It's warm.'

Tanya looked along the coverlet into his eyes. The ropes of hair almost covered her face. Her thumb came out with a sucking noise.

'Mark on my thumb,' she said.

'Show me.'

She held out the wet thumb.

'Don't you want to come in,' he lifted up the coverlet, 'a little bit?'

Tanya kicked off her shoes with a giggle and he felt her slide underneath.

'Oooh, *book* . . . ' She sat up and reached down the bed for it. Then she lay back and put her thumb in her mouth. Stephen put his arm round her.

'Friends now?'

Tanya nodded slowly, and he tightened his arm. She snuggled against him, turning the pages of the book, still nodding in slow, absent jerks of the head.

'Too hot in here,' she announced after a minute, pulling away and climbing out of bed. She patted the coverlet.

'Now, you just stay there and keep quiet like a good boy,' she assumed the tone of a nurse, 'because you aren't very well.'

He watched her through the bars as she moved to the door.

'Your book,' said Stephen faintly, but the click of the door drowned his words.

Beside him on the pillow, disturbed by the vibration of the bed, the book opened, its leaves flicking slower and slower until they came to rest at a dog-eared page. The heavy type caught his eye and he began to read:

Destroying Angel (*amanita virosa*) Contains amanitatoxins which destroy the nuclei of the liver cells and prevent protein synthesis. The kidneys too are subject to irreversible damage. The toxins of the Destroying Angel cause massive disorders of the digestive system, symptoms which may not appear for several days. Death occurs up to fourteen days after ingestion.
N.B. There is considerable risk of confusing the Destroying Angel with white edible mushrooms, especially in the button stage. In woodland be very careful in picking white fungi which are in an early stage of development.

LITTLE GOETHE

ONE

From time to time, a pencil sketch of a face emerges and fades at the french window. It occurs always in the same place: the penultimate pane in the right hand row.

The sky is blue. Somewhere on the road towards Tunbridge Wells a motor horn sounds, insistently. From my sand pit the blossom looks like braided ribbons of pink and white silk. I sit, crosslegged, holding a damp fistful of sand, staring open-mouthed at the shifting grains. Inside my head, the synapses of my brain are jammed, like city bridges in a rush hour, with electro-chemical traffic. The very serenity of this spring morning – the innocence of the leaves, the blandness of the house across the lawn – testifies to the arrival of the crisis. Have they seen through me at last? I feel it in my diminutive bones. I am getting careless these days, I am getting old. I can't remember my lines, my cues, my part so well.

I am Everard Sharpe. At least, that is what Caitlin and Gilbert call me. To all intents and purposes, I am eight years old. For the last seven years, I have been considered a prodigy. As soon as they discovered the extraordinary nature of the child they had adopted, Caitlin and Gilbert set out, with great determination and self-sacrifice, to create a set of circumstances – a uniquely rich soil – in which their precocious young orchid could be brought to early bloom. Such are the blind energies of sublimation.

With what nostalgia now I look round my study. My hand strays in an affectionate caress over the back of my old friend, the miniature leather armchair in which, at the tender age of two (it seems so long ago now) I sat, my legs dangling short of the Persian rug, to render lispingly the opening sentences of Thucydides' *Peloponnesian Wars*.

Later on, a special system of ladders was devised, fitted on brass runners that ran all around the room, so that I in my thirst for knowledge could ransack unaided the topmost shelves.

If only those days could return . . . What innocence. Every

morning, I used to play chameleons. After breakfast, a light collation of rusks and cream which I took alone, surrounded by the day's newspapers, in my cot, I invited Caitlin and Gilbert to choose for me at random a piece of English prose, precisely twelve hundred words in length – something, say, from Russell's *History of Western Philosophy*, or a choice piece of Gibbon perhaps. Entranced, I carried it – if it was small enough – into my study, where I translated it without pause through Greek, Latin, German, French and Italian, before retranslating it into English. If my final passage did not agree, strictly, word for word, with the original, I considered myself to have failed and started over again. I did not arrive at the coincidence of original and final passages by any act of memory. The whole virtue of the game was this: the language in which I finished – the world I finished by inhabiting – was not being *returned to*, but created anew; it was, in my protean eyes, merely one of many, merely the particular medium in which, joyful chameleon as I then was, I chose to bask.

My study is now only a friendly dinosaur. My digital computer has an information retrieval system capable of retaining ten times the knowledge that is stacked laboriously on its shelves. It rests on my bedside table.

My chessboard stands idle now, the ebony and ivory pieces cradled in their green baize graves. It is almost six years since the final of the World Infant Chess Championship in Belgrade. My opponent was Rechevsky, a scowling, heavily-fancied, one-year-old from the Ukraine. Strapped into our highchairs in the centre of the smoke-filled auditorium, we looked more like umpires in some other game than players in our own. I opened quietly, noticing the flicker of contempt which crossed Rechevsky's face. I knew from the press he had been studying my openings. He produced the expected Sicilian. As we exchanged ritual pawns at the third and fourth, he permitted himself to smile. At the fifth, he drew forth an accelerated *fianchetto*, an irresistible habit of quoting from his favourite Holzhausen-Tarrasch 1912. At the seventh, he castled, and still I had initiated no effective counter-strike. At the eighth, after showing some aggression, my bishop sidled away, apparently innocuously. Rechevsky relaxed and moved his knight up on the flank. My pawn threatened, and, entirely unprepared for what was to follow, he retreated his other knight. The tenth and crushing move came out of the blue: my sidling bishop suddenly removed the intervening pawn and held him in check. His plight was suddenly brought home to him. He had no choice but to take my bishop with his king, thus exposing it. For Rechevsky, Scylla and Charybdis finally hove into view. If now he used his pawn to get rid of my offending knight, his queen could be taken by mine; if he used his king again, he would be drawn into my mating-net. The game was effectively over in ten moves. At the twelfth, Rechevsky ignominiously surrendered his queen. White with disbelief, he was unstrapped from his chair and carried from the hall amid uproar. Rumour has it that so great was his pique, he has not yet acquired the art of speech.

Alas, those days are long since gone. A line of poetry now comes to seem like a recrimination. The more ancient, the more telling the judgment. Sometimes, I repeat to myself Virgil's immortal 'Sunt lacrimae rerum, et mentem mortalia tangunt' and in each of my eyes there rises – irrepressible, flecked with amber – a sea-green hemisphere. A precise degree of impersonal sadness: not a milli-litre less or more. My head bows. If ever those lines applied to a life, it is mine.

TWO

I was born in Vienna in 1898. My mother, Roma, was the by-blow of a brief encounter between a Slovenian peasant woman and a wealthy Triestine, a manufacturer of special paints for the hulls of ships. She was selling apples at a stall by the side of the road, when he happened to pass by. According to Roma, she offered him one, and the fateful transaction took place with all speed behind the stall. The analogy with the alleged mother of mankind was not lost on Roma's fertile imagination.

Roma early showed a talent for music and eventually, with the help of her father's discreet influence, found her way into the Vienna Conservatoire. Afterwards, she became a soprano at the

Opera House. A long-legged brunette with an inimitable swaying walk and coal-black eyes, she was very much in demand at salons and parties. She formed a series of liaisons with men of taste and substance and became rich.

She also became pregnant, though she would never tell me which one of the stream of visitors to our roomy apartment over-looking the Ringstrasse was my father. Ouf, cried Roma, her eyes waltzing with innuendo. Your little head will grow bigger than it is already. Then he is noble, I insisted, he is extraordinary. But her only reply was to slide mischievously into the chorale from the last scene of *Don Giovanni*, wrapping her seductive lips round the words and dropping into an outrageous Triestine accent:

> Where is the miscreant?
> Where is the criminal?
> Now shall our retribution
> Be unleashed

She was impossible, unpredictable; and for a few years, she won such a following, she was so fashionable, that she could do anything she pleased.

Roma loved to offend etiquette: she insisted on humping me through the crowded streets herself, a relic no doubt of her Balkan peasant blood. My first few words were echoes of the café repartee which Roma took such shameless advantage of. I lay impassive in my bassinette, or sat, skewered to a chair with her one gloved hand, while she flirted with the other across the table. I was appealed to, rhetorically at first, for my judgment in all matters from affairs of the heart to the minutiae of business strategy; soon, much to everyone's amusement except Roma's, I gave it. At six months I could read fluently in Italian and German. 'Little Goethe', they nicknamed me, those bewhiskered bankers and envious bohemians.

At first Roma loved it. She played up to her Little Goethe: she pouted with pride, her generous mouth puckering into a rosebud, whipping up applause everywhere for her portable oracle. But soon she realised that Little Goethe was beginning to steal her thunder. I was proving too much of an attraction on my own account. One day, I overreached myself. I corrected the waiter as to the amount of the bill. Consternation reigned; then roars of laughter broke out, as I was pronounced correct. Roma looked daggers. Herr Schneider, the stockbroker, leant across the table.

Roma, I heard him whisper, this little fellow is beginning to upstage you . . . why don't you let Professor Gruber have him . . . The child may have something wrong with him, do you take my meaning? If he doesn't, in any event I swear he will be a prodigy. He'll need sending away to a special school . . . He looks sickly to me . . . look how big his head is . . .

Some time after this conversation, a grave man with gigantic side-whiskers and a porcelain tulip in his buttonhole appeared at the door of the apartment and presented his card. Roma's eyes lit up when she saw the flower. Ah, Magyar, she said, a patriot is always welcome at my door, Herr Professor. Gruber advanced and kissed her hand. He drew himself up to his full height.

My mother, Erzebet Hatvany, he said solemnly, married Gruber the German in Budapest, much to my cost. He indicated his buttonhole. But this tariff war, believe me, is only the beginning of the end for this unfortunate Prussian attachment.

Immediately they fell into passionate anticipation of the fall of the Hapsburg Empire. In her less self-conscious moments, Roma thought of herself as an Irredentist. I knew better; her so-called nationalism was founded on one thing. Roma had her eyes on Milan. She dreamt of herself, the Trieste dispute finally settled, taking La Scala by storm: the bella figura of a reunified Italy. She quoted Mazzini and Garibaldi by the yard. Passionately, she picked up the newspaper. Even that fool Nigra, the Italian ambassador, is saying that Austria's policy is nothing more than effacement.

Gruber replied with a first-hand account of the funeral of Louis Kossuth, the Hungarian patriot, instancing the atrocities of the Austrian troops; he finished by quoting in resonant Hungarian the prophetic warning of Kossuth on his deathbed, to the effect that the Hapsburgs were doomed, and unless she broke away Hungary also would perish in the flames.

They immediately cemented their alliance by going to the piano and singing, their arms firmly wrapped about one another, a round of Liszt's peasant melodies, interspersed with Italian marching songs.

The result of this mutual rhapsody was that later in the day I found myself in a fiacre, lying on red plush, being addressed on all manner of subjects by Professor Gruber. I didn't like the turn events had taken. The politics of the situation were delicate. Tempting as it was, the possibility of answering plainly and truth-fully the questions he put to me was out of the question. If I did that, I should endanger my credibility as a prodigy, by appearing far too advanced. I did not know what the exact consequences of 'appearing as I was' would be, but instinctively I felt they would be awkward and unpleasant: I should almost certainly have to leave Roma. On the other hand, if I didn't respond at all, he would conclude that I was either a perfectly ordinary child, or even a dull one. This was infinitely preferable as a stratagem, but I knew it wouldn't work. Gruber's opinion would simply be discarded by Roma: she knew that I was neither of these. She would almost certainly seek a second opinion. I should have to go through it all again. No, I reasoned, the only course of action which would foil Roma was to present myself as an uninteresting, second-rate sort of child prodigy, of the kind that are two-a-penny in any society at any time. This would satisfy both of them; and it would give her some badly-needed ammunition with which to discredit me in front of the crowd at Schmidts. Gruber's questions, I determined, were to be answered by an instructive pattern of errors.

In the swaying carriage he ordered me to watch him carefully. Then he proceeded to put his hands together, fingers interlocked, and squeeze them one against the other close to my ear. They squelched loudly (he had exceedingly moist palms).

Now, said Gruber, smoothing his moustache, pay the closest possible attention. Look at my hands . . . is there anything in them? He spread them, like a conjurer, under my nose. They reeked of carbolic soap and something else I had not smelt before. I looked up at him and shook my head. Then, said Gruber triumphantly, what is *that*? He squelched them again, close to my ear. I closed my eyes, giving the impression, I hoped, of one deep in confusion; a tiny brain, wrestling with a completely new phenomenon. I decided to risk it so far. Air, I said cautiously. And where does this 'air' come from, said Gruber. I appeared to think for a moment. In reality, I was repressing an impulse to throw caution to the winds and crush this insulting, patronising line of questioning once and for all. The voice of intellectual honesty rose strong and clear in my head: 'The pressure of your hands,' it declared with bell-like clarity, 'pushes out the air, causing a vacuum. Aided by your excessive and disgusting sweat, your palms then adhere to one another. As you then relax your hands and allow an opening to appear, air rushes back into the vacuum, which, as every schoolboy knows, Nature abhors.'

The moment passed. I had overcome the temptation. I opened my eyes and looked around. It's everywhere, I said. Does it come from beneath the carriage? said Gruber. I swallowed. Who knows where this labyrinth might lead? I nodded.

Ha, shouted Gruber. Could my hands make that noise if there were no air in the carriage? Again, I paused and frowned in apparent concentration. Integrity urged again, with the clarity of a loudhailer: 'Certainly not, for then there would be no air, initially, for your palms to displace.' Again, with considerable effort, I ignored it. Yes, I said. Why, pounced Gruber. Because, I said, inwardly groaning at my corruption, air could still come in through the hole. I pointed at a gap in the floor, through which the road could be seen rushing by. Gruber smiled and took out his pad.

A discussion followed on the nature of my respiratory system, in which I resolutely emptied my mind of as many of its assumptions as I could manage. Shamelessly, I claimed to have no lungs. I suggested that air was attracted in some mysterious way to my mouth as I spoke. To do this, I had to suppress whole paragraphs of Harvey's treatise on the circulation of the blood which appeared, as if on a lighted screen, before my eyes. Before long, I had embarked on a medieval view of my anatomy and physiology.

The conversation broke off when we drew up at Gruber's school in the Wekerlestrasse. We climbed several flights of stairs – Gruber and the coachman, that is, in whose burly arms I was cradled – and entered a large room. There I was put down in a sea of white-shawled hopefuls like myself. From the walls a gaggle of parents, natural and adopted, began to call out instructions to their off-spring. As we entered the room, the racket diminished slightly and a momentary hush fell on the company; it was then that I realised what a powerful man my inquisitor was. He disappeared through a door, leaving me lying helpless amongst them.

Everywhere I could hear their growling voices; all round me I sensed the rustle of their frail intellects, as they crawled heavily over one another like worms in a jar, issuing challenges. Before I could protest, I was jammed in a fetid corner between two of them. One thrust his (or her, it was difficult to tell) milky, jowled face into mine and challenged me to a duel of quadratic equations. Best of three, it leered.

I declined as politely as I could, for I didn't wish to draw attention to myself. Callisthenics my friend, I murmured, do not appeal to me. Then the creature on the other side puffed up its already swollen cheeks like a toad, and offered to blow me out of the room with Mozart's horn concerto.

What a flea circus! What blind, crawling mechanisms of human vanity! I pitied them, that crowd of force-fed mountebanks, as they bawled out their cheapjack wares, their *tricks*, with insolent rivalry. Yet I was forced to impersonate one of them; and I was already having such miserable success that even the tutored eye of Gruber could not distinguish me from them. For a moment, I was shaken: supposing he never returned. Appearance would close over reality, like the lid over a coffin.

I surveyed the crew round the walls, and my confidence returned. I read in their faces the long tale of food withheld, sleep interrupted, the driving, distorting pressure to achieve their primitive, vicarious goals. But with confidence came a new awareness of my isolation. How could I have explained to anyone that the only goal my mind ever needed or acknowledged was an enlightened form of self-perception? My mind unfolds – sweetly, incessantly – within its own proportions by spontaneous applications of pure reason. My curiosity, insatiable in all things, is satisfied ultimately by the agency of what appears to be a superior act of memory.

I had at that time recently arrived, without any form of outside consultation beyond the execution by humming of a modest piece of Palestrina (a favourite lullaby of Roma's), at an embryonic version of the theory of polyphony, a theory which had taken, according to the vagaries of historical process, some seven centuries to evolve. I was already reaching the stage of predicting – again, without consulting dictionaries or histories of music – some of the less complex developments of the Renaissance and Baroque eras.

How could I have explained this to a horn-blowing toad?

Fortunately, such a herculean task was not required of me, for Gruber reappeared. He clapped his hands and informed everyone that the school would be closed for a week.

As soon as the last of them was out of the massive front door, Gruber locked it decisively. I was left squatting alone, rafted on my shawl in a vast expanse of parquet, trying to prevent the relief from showing on my face. Then for a week he went to work on me.

The first few days were taken up with a meticulous physiological examination. He took me into his laboratory. Over the door was a large placard, placed as if to remind him of something. It read:

BEWARE OF PERSEVERATION!

Crooning snatches of a Magyar ballad, he stripped me of my swaddling clothes and laid me on the table. For three days, he pored over me, making frantic notes on a pad by his side. When he came to my vertebrae, he muttered and sighed and shook his head, as if all was lost. He prised open my mouth, counted my teeth, and shone his torch down my throat. Then he seemed to get absorbed in something down there. He drew in his breath, and felt my neck on the outside. My skull he took gently in his hands, as if it were a piece of delicate china, inspected it, and weighed it thoughtfully. Then he put me upright in a padded clamp and read off all kinds of measurements.

Each morning he resumed his restless catechism. But by now I had become more skilled in negotiating the rapids of interrogation, spicing my replies with exactly the degree of intellectual solecism which he wanted to hear. As we were driving along one morning after breakfast, Gruber noticed a cloud in the sky. He pointed to it and asked me if it was moving. I said that it was. What made it move, he asked. *We* did, I answered. He immediately stopped the carriage and we walked into the park. He propped me on a bench. The cumulo-nimbus drifted fleecily, peacefully by. It cannot be us, he said, slyly, for now we are still. Ah, said I, but look over there at the bustling street. Others are moving. Ha, said Gruber, we shall see. He got up and bundled me into the carriage. We drove out towards Aspern and stopped and walked into the middle of a flat field. There were no people to be seen, except ourselves. In the sky hung a single raincloud. Now, said Gruber. We waited. It remained exactly where it was. Get on, said Gruber under his breath. We waited another five minutes. The cloud remained stationary in the middle of the sky. We walked back to the carriage, Gruber visibly upset. When we reached the carriage, we turned to look for a last time at the cloud. It was almost out of sight, hastening across the sky, as if to some appointment for which it was late. You see, said Gruber, it has moved. Ah, said I, but so have we. Clicking his tongue furiously, he almost threw me into the carriage and reached for his pad.

On the way back to Vienna, we passed a lake. We stopped. He held me up at the side of the open carriage. You see the lake, he said, what is it? I told him it was water. Do you see it move? he asked. There are waves, I said, lapping at the edges. Why are the waves only at the edges, he asked. I paused. He prodded me. Is it because they are naughty? he asked. I smiled scornfully. If that were the reason, I replied, there would come a time when the lake got tired of punishing them, and they would all go back to the middle again, but they don't travel in that direction. Then why *do* the waves move? said Gruber, his nose somewhat out of joint. Because the lake is getting ready for the boats, I said. He looked across at the water for some time in silence. Then, he rounded on me, his finger held high. The boats, he cried, are all moored. Yes, I replied, but the boatmen are on their way.

Immediately he ordered the coachmen to drive on. After the cloud incident, I had the suspicion he did not wish to risk the appearance of any boatmen.

Sometimes we drifted into what amounted to a reversal of roles, though Gruber didn't seem to notice this. One day, when we came in sight of the river, he caught me in his arms and ran across the grass down the embankment to the towpath. He took out his red silk handkerchief and threw it into the water. As the handkerchief drifted off, he asked me which way was the river flowing. When I told him, he asked me what made it move? By now, Gruber was becoming disingenuous. Without waiting for a response, he proposed that the movement of the water was caused by great unseen fish, fanning it along with their tails. He watched me closely. Then why couldn't we see them, I asked in a hectoring, inquisitorial way. Oh, he replied, airily, they were swimming too deep. I thought for a moment; since he had started to parody me, the most effective tactic I could adopt, the natural course of action, was for me to impersonate him. I asked him, in the manner of a legal counsel, if he saw the anglers along the bank. He replied that he did. Would the river not go slower, I asked, if many of the fish in it were caught? Perhaps, I suggested, sarcastically, if all the fish in the river were taken out, it would stop flowing altogether . . .

For a moment, I thought my hubris was going to bring a fall. He looked at me, considering my words with a frown on his face. Then an expression of great peace came over his features and he wrote, happily, in his notebook: 'Fifth stage!!!' etc.

When finally we returned to the apartment, we found Roma lying, propped against a bank of monogrammed pillows, sifting through the reviews of her maiden performance of the new operatic sensation, *La Bohème*. Gruber dumped me rudely in an armchair and made a rush for the doors of her bedroom, closing them ineffectually behind him, such was his passion. Raising my head with the utmost difficulty over the arm of the chair, I could just see him kneeling at her bedside, fervently clasping her hand. I strained to hear, but I could catch only fragments of their dialogue '. . . of the utmost gravity,' I heard him say, looking back towards me over his shoulder. 'Sick?' said Roma. 'Is he going to . . . '

'Far from it,' said Gruber, ' . . . an embarrassing length of time . . . '

'For *ever*?' shouted Roma. 'Have you taken leave of your senses?'

'The body chemistry is quite unique . . . the thymus is enormously enlarged and appears to be ducted . . . '

'What are you talking about?'

'We are unsure of the function of this gland, but it is normally considered to be vestigial . . . it withers away after childhood in normal individuals, but in your son it shows no sign of doing so. Quite the contrary, my dear lady, it is highly active . . . it is, if you will pardon the metaphor, the conductor of his body orchestra, slowing down his pulse rate to a quite extraordinary degree . . . everything including the thyroid and pituitary glands is performing a perfectly regular *andante* movement . . . '

'Yes but what does this mean?'

'I don't know. I have never encountered anything like this before . . . it seems unlikely that he will grow to normal adult size though his brain is already that of a precocious boy of ten . . . '

Here I breathed a sigh of relief. At least my strategy had worked. But I had reckoned without my physiology. 'His size,' Gruber went on, 'is difficult to predict . . . but unless some glandular *allegro* takes place, which could be fatal of course, he'll probably be something in between a large infant and an underdeveloped boy. It's all quite fascinating. His head is already too large for his neck muscles to support properly and he may need some kind of neck brace . . . '

'Oh,' cried Roma, sinking back amongst the pillows and dabbing at her eyes with a black lace handkerchief. 'What am I going to do? He's a . . . monster!' In a sudden fit of belated delicacy, Gruber went to the door and shut it, and I heard no more, except the *basso continuo* of his assurances, broken occasionally by a trill of renewed tears.

For three days, Roma locked herself in her room and refused entry to all comers. Her latest beau was turned away. She ate nothing. On the fourth day, the jasperine handles of the double doors were flung open and she emerged, dressed in a cascade of yellow silk flounces and holding a parasol, her face wreathed in smiles. With a squeal of joy, she ran to the damasked armchair where I was lying more or less as Gruber had dumped me and snatched me to her. Ah, Putsi, my darling, she cried, what must you think of your Roma? Her voice purred in its lowest register as she planted kisses on both my cheeks. How could I leave you alone for so long, eh? The room spun below as she whirled me high in the air. My little Roma had a plan, she explained to me as we waltzed together down the Ringstrasse and settled ourselves at our sunny table at Schmidts.

The tactics were familiar to me. The more sensitive the issue, the more public the airing it had to have. When she began to outline her idea, her finger gaily crooked round the handle of a coffee cup, I objected. We rowed; goggling, a crowd gathered round our table. In the end, the commotion grew too much even for Roma. She picked me up and we continued in the Heldenplatz. I begged her to retain me. I asked her to put pressure on Gruber to forget about me. If she was not prepared to look after me, could she not hire someone? I was even prepared to go to a special school or a hospital. She said they had discussed it. Gruber had insisted that it was her duty to hand me over to medical science. He had hinted that he would blacken her reputation. She had refused, she said, to condemn me to the life of a guinea pig. Even as she spoke, I admired her. She was magnificent, heroic. I said I would rather go to a madhouse. I instanced all the poets and seers and political prisoners I could think of who had languished in jails and insane asylums, and yet had retained some vision, some indestructible inner life. I would rather be like them, I said. It would not have to come to that, said Roma, hugging me to her.

We came to the statue of Prince Eugene of Savoy. The morning sun lit the epaulettes of the figure; cast from the prancing, imperial charger, a set of spiked shadows menaced the pavement. We stood in them. Equally, she said, she was sure she could not give me what I needed. That was why she had hit upon her plan. It was the only way. How did she know what I needed, I argued desperately. Putsi darling, said Roma, I shall be leaving Vienna soon. I tire of entertaining these Prussian fools. I am going to Milan. Schneider will fix it so I can get Italian nationality. I shall be free at last. I cannot wait, my dear, for Italia to be redeemed, I must redeem her myself.

As she tossed her head, I smelt the freshness of the city, the sun wiping the last remnants of dew from the cobbles, the crisp sound of the cabs going round the square. I realised suddenly that this was our farewell scene: she, absurdly vain, operatically proud, pirouetting in the shadow of the statue; I, close to her hair, begging and whining in her ear, gazing imploringly into her face.

It was, in fact, not the last time I saw her, though I prefer to think of it as the last. On April 30th, 1918, I was on my way to a physics conference in Interlaaken. My train had a long wait at Milan. I looked up from the notes I was making and gazed, idly, across the platform; it was crowded with soldiers of every nationality. My attention was arrested by the coarse-featured, grey-haired woman who had emerged from the bar. She was carrying a drunken soldier on her back in a fireman's lift. She brought him to some steps almost opposite my carriage window and tumbled him off her shoulders like a sack of potatoes. Then she dusted off her hands and stood, arms akimbo, glaring down at him with a mixture of contempt and satisfaction, which began to seem strangely familiar to me. Picking the crumbs of shortcake from my velvet suit, I got down from the wagon-lit to have a closer look. Beneath that barrel shape, could it be her? As my foot touched the platform, I heard her break into an ironical phrase from *Carmen*: the cracked voice a shadow of itself, retaining only its bravura. Behind me, I felt the train begin to move. I was racked by the impulse to dash over to her and throw myself, blindly, into her arms. Almost involuntarily, I stepped back on to the running-board of the carriage. As we slid by, I saw her disappear into the smoke-filled bar. Through the grimy panes, I could see her upright form threading its way through the crowded uniforms to the counter. My eye caught the flourish of scrolled letters over the door: La Scala.

I scarcely felt the breeze on my face, the lurch of the points, as we rolled out through the marshalling-yards, the hands drawing me back inside the train. The only feeling I had gripped me through and through: it was as if the twenty years in between did not exist. I really was at last irrevocably lost to Roma, and she to me. From now on, I breathed only the oxygen of her plan.

THREE

Roma set up a trust, to be administered indefinitely, to finance The Genetrix Adoption Society, whose sole purpose was to get me adopted by a succession of the most gullible, childless, wealthy parents to be found. She foresaw that things being as they were with me, I should require, not merely one set of future parents, but an indefinite number. Who knew when I should die? Meanwhile between situations (she said she knew the feeling, having often been between shows herself) I should need to be taken care of until I could be found a new home. The situation was the reverse of normal: usually, she explained, childhood was the transient factor, and parents were stable; but I should be permanent, and my parents ephemera.

So it has turned out. The only constant is me, and my needs. Flesh perishes, I live on. The officials of the Genetrix, who receive me back after each life, pass away in due course; the financiers who administer the trust lay their heads low in charming cemeteries, snug beneath the snow line of the majestic Swiss Alps; but, like the money in whose service they expire, I go on from decade to decade, from family to family. Written instructions accompany me, handed down from generation to generation, for security's sake.

Throughout all its local changes of situation, I retain one abstract impression about my life: nothing has changed, despite appearances to the contrary. Roma's plan is an archetype which, existing outside time, devours its particular manifestations. It has even spread its tentacles backwards, before it existed, to my real origins, and they have been subsumed into it. Roma herself has become a mere character in the story she began by inventing. Even as she explained the plan to me, I recognised her ambition. Here was a strategy which exceeded in wit, in panache, all her operatic roles. Here, she was not merely a performer, a lackey to the conceptions of others, but the prime mover of a life, a multitude of lives. But the opera has escaped its dimensions; it has turned upon its authoress in a casting session she never bargained for: now, as I begin to recall her bounce of delight at her own ingenuity, the image converts itself into an anterior scene; her conversation freezes into dialogue; her beseechings spiral into arias; and (what might have been a memory as real as time itself) her jewelled fingers, flashing eloquently in the spring sunlight, reflect only the spotlight in a crowded auditorium.

For this reason, I do not propose to give a chronology of my travels since I left her, replete with local colour, dates, faces, accents, and incidents. Declaiming the list in its temporal order would be as meaningless as writing out all the figures in a recurring decimal. I will content myself with stating the theme: it contains in posse most of its variations.

But how could I pose as an infant plausibly enough to take in the searching visions of couple after couple? The answer to this is woefully simple. People who are looking for something badly enough, are usually prepared to find it at the earliest convenient opportunity. The Genetrix specialises in convenient opportunities. Commonsense leads one to expect that self-interest would interfere with the process of acceptance. It is not so: I, as no other, can testify. Had the Genetrix monitored its activities, we should find some remarkably similar patterns of behaviour on the part of prospective parents. They would have the banality of a list of religious conversions. Where the experience is emotionally absolute, the stereotypes appear to be strongest. The infant life is the very centre of other people's self-projection. When the cipher 'infant' is held up before them, they see not what is there, but what they want to see. The infant is the most conventionalised object of perception in human life. Naturally, the figures per annum for baby-switches in our major hospitals are not available; but it is well-known that the mother, who has carried this burden within her for nine long months, who has sweated and laboured to bring it into the world, often has no means of recognising it as an individual, and is quite contented with the baby of another.

The Genetrix Adoption Society presents me in thoroughly conventionalised form. Care is taken that I am never seen in the context of other children. Parents are, if possible, selected for their inexperience. Childless parents – inexperienced in matching their own imaginative projections with the schema 'baby' – fall like ninepins. My size, in fact, has never changed throughout my long career. I have simply graduated my dress, posture, verbal and general behaviour, to accord with their rampant expectations. Swathed in my diapers and covered by a shawl, I instantly become an infant of piquant ugliness. My voice – since I have never breasted the tape of puberty – is a falsetto anyway. My withered member, untroubled throughout all these years by tumescence, passes credibly enough for an organ in its infancy, which, in a sense, it is.

The prospective parents, carefully vetted by the Genetrix for income, property, intelligence, lifestyle etc., arrive at, say, the Paris office. I am displayed, asleep. They approach to get their first view of me. I open my eyes, see them, and immediately begin to cry – a tiny, pathetic, strangled wail. By reflex the mother-to-be reaches out to quell the bawling she believes herself to have occasioned. Instantly, she finds, to her surprise and delight, she has done so. My timing is precise. The ensuing smile is so spontaneous it is hard for her to resist the impression of cause and effect. The belief that she will be a good mother begins to fulfil itself before her very eyes.

There have been one or two variations on this. In 1938, for example, on meeting the Countess Ouspensky in Rome, I vomited a quantity of milk over her sable coat and crushed her lorgnette in my tiny fists. These actions were carefully rehearsed, of course; it was well-known that the Countess already had considerable experience of fraudulent adoption. Her conventions were quite different. After months of study, the Genetrix's research committee, headed by Otto Schlesinger, decided that the most effective policy would be to simulate intransigence. Their calculations were quite correct: she saw me as the Infant Hercules, and her Nietzschean predilections were charmed and titillated. I was assured – thanks to the care with which this operation was carried out – of a serene five years in her *palazzo* overlooking the Forte di Belvedere in Florence; a period during which (despite the rigours of war) I conceived and executed my famous essay 'Objections to Behaviourism'.

But by far the most daring coup of this kind took place in the Daytona Nursing Home in Dayton, Ohio, in September 1948.

There the twenty-three stone Mrs Grace Metallika, a millionairess from Cuyahoga County, was, in the presence of her husband Walter, delivered prematurely of a foetus of enormous size, which appeared to be alive and well. The Metallikas were delighted with me; and I lived with them quite happily on their farm for four and a half years before they were both tragically killed in an automobile accident on the Cleveland Freeway. Otto had long wished to pull off something of this order. When the news leaked out that Mrs Metallika would miscarry, he seized his chance. The Genetrix carefully infiltrated the nursing home; all the staff were lavishly primed; the media were invited. On the morning of September 13th, Mrs Metallika was secretly delivered by Caesarian section of her premature baby – a tiny foetus which was, as expected, still-born. I was then inserted in place of it – 'an interesting problem in heavy mechanics,' said the gynaecological surgeon, Mr Raymond Spygold. For forty-five minutes I lay in the hot, slimy folds of Mrs Metallika's recently-vacated womb, the cords of the departed foetus attached to my navel by a rubber sucker, breathing through a plastic tube which descended over the neck of the cervix and protruded at the vagina. Then Mr Metallika was called in to watch the final stages as I was triumphantly 'delivered' by Caesarian section, the surgeon merely cutting his own stitches and sewing them up again.

This impersonation of homunculus is an exception; but in general the periodic regression to babyhood is quite repugnant to me. To lie, immobile as a man in an iron lung, in a state of deliberately induced bodily incontinence, imitating the truncated motor responses, the wild, bullying eye-movements of infancy, is not an edifying experience. These early days are a trial; I dread them like a punishment each time they come round. Were I remotely interested in power, I should no doubt find them intensely satisfying. My slightest wish is no sooner hinted at, than it is performed, with cooing servitude. Unfortunately the amount of wishes I am allowed to have, according to the laws of conventional expectation, are few indeed and limited in their range. Choice is not a great feature of a baby's life, even though one is expected to be inherently manipulative at this stage, and conduct the orchestra of one's admirers by tiny, jerky movements of the hands.

The basic helplessness of this period is illustrated by my brief stay in 1911 on the Isle of Sylt, at the summer home of Herr and Frau Albrecht, a Bavarian timber contractor and his wife. Frau Albrecht became anxious: I didn't seem to be doing very well on the bottled milk she was giving me (I was of course an enormous

One morning they brought in Grüss-Gott, a local girl. With a sigh of relief, she unstrapped herself; her bosoms flopped in front of her like stretched gourds. I looked at them as I was taken on to her knee: the skin was satin with pressure; each blue nipple, leaking already like a village pump, rose decisively from its plateau of coconut-matting. Frau Albrecht was smiling and nodding in the background. Before I could cry out, Grüss-Gott caught me by the back of the neck and squeezed the nearest of these machines, like a fire-extinguisher, into my mouth, which happened to be gaping with astonishment. For several hours afterwards, I lay in a sticky coma, horribly real to me, but interpreted as a benign satisfied nap by the Albrechts. The process was repeated for weeks.

At this stage I am like a man in prison, not even able to count the days in scratches on the walls of his cell; for counting, like language, is forbidden me. It is the worst form of political imprisonment: I am deprived of all human rights; I am woken every three or four hours, just when my eyes are finally closing in sleep, and forced to drink a sweet-tasting liquid, which leaves me drowsy and sluggish. I am got up. I am bounced up and down. I am struck repeatedly on the back, until I have an uncontrollable fit of belching and vomiting. My eyes stare up into an electric light. Voices whisper in my ears. Then I am put down and left alone in the pitch dark until this process is repeated four hours later.

But infinitely worse than the physical torment is the mental and spiritual deprivation. My mind, like a fire, burns for fuel; it consumes only itself. I can feel it fading, dying down; yet I force myself to hang on, to wait until the embers of my intelligence can be revived by the kindling of babble; then, cautiously, the first dry sticks of sentences. It is a slow process, fraught with anxiety, and in the meantime, often, I have the torment, as I am dandled on their knees, of hearing the second-hand, inaccurate opinions of my current elders. Patiently I sit, beaming, the saliva depending in a thread from my bottom lip, enduring statements of prejudice and ignorance, confidently delivered over a vast range of subjects. Sometimes they speak of the latest developments in the literary or scientific worlds; yet in such a fragmented and muddled fashion that I weep, loudly, in front of them, out of sheer despair.

Fortunately after a month of two I can begin to leak information concerning my development, in such a way as to secure an early impression of intelligence. Here I must be careful: the impression must not be too strong, the intelligence not too great, or the credibility of the whole operation may be jeopardised. This requires two quite contradictory qualities: great self-discipline, and a thoroughly corrupt imagination. The Genetrix – though examining carefully the susceptibilities of each set of parents – does not present me as a child prodigy. It is left entirely up to me to engineer this impression. How much I choose to reveal of myself is therefore entirely my own responsibility. Obviously the more of myself I can reveal, the nearer I approach the life I would have led, had all things been equal. It is a radiant hypothesis which conditions my every thought and action. Not that I am not free in this matter. I would not indulge in sentiment. But to have to raise the house of one's personality on the quicksand of calculated misunderstanding, when one has a vision as clear as mine of what living on a rock might be, creates an ineradicable reflex of frustration.

The next stage involves, mercifully, the beginnings of mobility and articulacy. Here I can liken my condition most closely to that of a man recovering from a severe automobile accident which has damaged his mind and body almost beyond repair, but not quite. My elders wait on the slightest signs of convalescence. I strain to achieve the sitting position, usually over a period of three or four days; they strain with me. When I finally achieve it, there is an air of celebration. They dress me in different clothes; things more suitable for one who can sit up and begin to join the human race. I am at last becoming one of them. I climb perilously on to the hood of my pram, or show signs of balancing on the rails of my cot. I am rewarded by being allowed to crawl on the ground and inhabit a kind of wooden exercise-yard. I am dressed in trousers. When the time comes, I am congratulated on my lack of incontinence. The unintelligible syllables I mumble are greeted by prolonged applause and imitation. Esperanto, I find, sufficiently badly-pronounced, is a good medium to use at this stage in most European countries; it also acts as a welcome salve to my injured dignity.

But how can I possibly simulate natural processes of growth? The acquisition of teeth, for example, is not a matter of convention. A creature either has them, or not: unconscious collusion cannot get rid of this fact. It is upon the consideration of details such as this that the success of the Genetrix rests. For this, Roma takes no credit; a stickler for detail in her own performances, she waved it aside in those of others. Otto and myself went over this very point, before launching me on my first household. We evolved a system which, after a certain amount of trial and error, has proved crudely effective. I get a signal out to the Genetrix; their representative then calls at the house on some pretext or other to slip me my first set of plates. There is a graduated set of these teething gums, made by a Swiss dental engineer, with one, two, three, and four milk teeth, embedded in minute top and bottom plates. The teeth are detachable, but may be secured by a tiny bolt, no bigger than a pinhead. This device helps me to simulate the emergence of a tooth overnight, without having to change my plate.

This whole part of the operation is not without its problems. The Genetrix employs a number of out-of-work actors to impersonate a whole range of callers. Their performances are at times quite indistinguishable from the real thing. Sometimes it happens (through failure of communication) that I am not aware which caller the representative will pose as. Once, isolated in a large house outside Lyon, I began to get desperately beyond my time for teething. With every day that passed, my credibility went down a point. Impatience was beginning to make me tense and nervous. Through the window, I saw a man arriving with a sack of logs on his back. I looked hard at him. Something about his face, some shade of incongruity in his walk, told me that here at last was my man. Even as I threw caution to the winds and slipped out of my pram, I remember pausing to admire the veracity of his performance. What an accurate impersonation. I followed him down the cellar steps, ignoring the hordes of skeletal green frogs which were hopping everywhere over the damp floor. Astonishing, he was even keeping it up when no one was looking. And that coarse grunt of relief as he threw down the sack. Quite impressive. I stood and faced him, halfway up the steps, in my diapers and tiny cotton nightshirt. OK, I said, holding out my palm, hand them over. He stared like a man in a Fuseli painting. For God's sake, I said, I haven't time for drama. I'll see you get a good reference. Just give me the teeth, will you. Then he fell, babbling hysterically, to his knees amongst the bobbing frogs. The function of this part of the act escaped me. It's all right, I said, no one's watching us now. At last, with a show of reluctance, he took from his mouth a set of top and bottom plates. A cunning hiding place, too, his own mouth. I swarmed back upstairs to my room. As I went, I made a mental note to write a special commendation of this man. He was a ham, but he was good. To my surprise, when I prepared to insert the teeth into my mouth, I discovered that they did not fit. They were crammed with inferior imitations of adult molars. One week later, the real agent arrived disguised – the cliché of it – as a gas inspector.

This affair of the teething has further ramifications in the parent's psychology of acceptance than one might expect from a rather cheap, mechanical ruse. If I am visibly teething, it is apparently more difficult to resist the probability that I am developing in other ways too. This makes it easier for me to give the impression of a marked precocity, for it becomes obvious that my speech is outstripping my ordinary physiological development. It is often remarked, for example, that my powers of articulacy are astonishing, given the fact that I have only just acquired my first tooth. This serves as a springboard for the most elevated of the delusions under which my adopted parents labour: the more remarkable my development, the more likely it is to have been caused by the environment and opportunities they have provided. Indispensable to the success of my fraud is the widespread superstition amongst parents that they themselves contribute directly to the growth and development of their offspring.

There is of course a spectrum in this. Some, like Mr Wolff, see themselves as contributing nothing more than material comfort: they are the hardest to deceive. Others believe – despite over-whelming evidence to the contrary – that they have created me *ex nihilo* (or *ex minimo*): examples of these include M. and Mme Sauvy, the botanists of Lyon, and Caitlin and Gilbert.

But no matter how great their belief in their own contribution, it is always open to me to betray myself. One afternoon, I remember, at the age of six months, I was playing with some large educational beads downstairs in the sitting room here at Caitlin and Gilbert's house. Gilbert was watching the TV. I had just finished assembling a model of the DNA nucleus, a little joke of mine to relieve the boredom; I happened to look up from under the arm of the chair at the screen. It was a silent film (how well I recall them when they first came out); a man was being pursued by some gangsters along the top of a skyscraper. He came to the edge, waved his arms, and fell off. The next shot showed him halfway down the skyscraper, hanging on to the minute-hand of a large clock, which was slowly buckling into a half-past position under his weight. My laugh (quite different in essence from my pseudo-laugh) burst out a split second before Gilbert's. He looked across at me suspiciously. I stretched and forced my mouth open in a grin, put my head back, and laughed again, hoping this would cover my *faux pas*. Unfortu-nately, at that very moment, the director cut to a vertiginous shot of the ant-like pedestrians, forty storeys below. My laugh (my cover-laugh) coincided with the canned laughter of the TV audience. Caitlin, said Gilbert, come in here a moment. He didn't take his eyes off me. I decided to patrol the room on all fours and create a diversion under the table. Look at him, said Gilbert, he just laughed at the TV. I came out from under the table, pushing out my tongue and rolling my eyes like an epileptic. I tell you, Gilbert insisted, he just got the joke. They watched me. Desperately I looked around. On the mantel was an alarm clock. I pointed to it. That's it, said Caitlin. Yes, they nodded in concert. Yes, it's the same isn't it? Same, I repeated with a sigh of relief. I could have sworn, said Gilbert. Isn't he sweet, said Caitlin, scooping me up with the little cry she reserved for my disappointing moments.

Then come the intelligence tests; the interviews with various overqualified members of the medical and psychiatric professions; scenes for which Gruber was an effective dress rehearsal. Usually by that time – nine months onward – special provisions have been made for my precocious aptitudes. I can spend some of my time 'reading'. Most of it, of course, pure show. I sit, a little later on, turning the pages of an elementary textbook, or reel off solutions to problems of specific gravity, while my mind rages with boredom and frustration at the thought of the printed matter which has poured from the world's presses since I was last able to peruse it.

At this stage, so greedy are the expectations I have aroused, that my parents sometimes begin to hallucinate meanings into my speech. In his conservatory at Lyon, while I was imitating as best I could the noises and gesticulations of a toddler, M. Sauvy suddenly formed the impression that I had uttered the name of a certain exotic plant. He begged me to repeat it. Much to my regret (it would have made things much easier for me at that stage) I could not. On another occasion, I was playing a game of chess with Gilbert, when my mind was struck by a particularly interesting thought. Rapt by the avenue of ratiocination that had opened up, I let fall from my nerveless fingers the piece I was holding. It dropped on an empty square, creating a checkmate. Gilbert was stunned and gratified in equal proportions. Like a child he set up the pieces again, expecting me to repeat it. This is a crucial moment: instead of the parent's favourite trick of losing deliberately, I have to accommodate myself to the reverse: I have to start winning ineptly in order to reassure the parents that I am humouring them. In many of these situations, the casual observer would not be able to tell the difference.

But when all these perils have been negotiated, then at last I enter the garden of delights. Soon my actual work is unintelligible to everyone around me. It is accepted that I am engaged in some important pursuit or other, but no one could tell, if asked, whether I am making sunbeams from cucumbers or designing a new hydrogen bomb. The strain becomes less, the frustration diminishes.

Serenity and happiness enter my life like long-lost friends. Sunlight falls through the panes of my study window, while I sit at my desk, my mind staccato with undreamt-of projects, finishing off the ones I have already conceived.

In the foreground of my mind, I gambol on an infinite green, as unselfconscious as a spring lamb. My activities are sheer superfluity: I perform effortless conceptual handsprings, out of sheer elation. But at the back of my mind, I know it is all a race against time. This halcyon period varies in length; but, allowing for accidents, fire, acts of God etc., on average somewhere between the ages of seven and ten, comes first the premonition, and then the certainty, that it is over for another life. This fragile causeway I am entered on at this moment; already, as I sit in this garden trowelling vigorously in the sand, I see the wave-caps of future lives obliterating the horizon.

The next stage – imminent now – is the rejection scene. In however many languages, cultures, accents, intonations, nuances, they always say the same things. You betrayed us, they shout, betrayed our trust. They begin to speak in the past tense of their love for me. Like so many caricatures of Pygmalion, they call my attention to the effort they have put into me; as if I were a painting that had gone on strike and walked out of its frame, or a statue that had got down from its pedestal and thumbed its nose at them. And what (applying the principle of *quid pro quo* which is all this bluster about love amounts to) have I ever given them in return? Anxiety. Waste of money.

At this point in their recriminations, I begin to feel like a zoo, whose unique animal stock – guaranteed to draw crowds, zoologists, media, study centres, the whole supporting structure of zoological life – turns out to have been founded on a few stray cats and local mongrels got up to look like tropical exotica; or myself, perhaps, stumbling down a concealed alley between the cages, changing from one wig and skin to another as I go.

I do not wish to enter into descriptions of how this comes about; it is as conventional and far from the truth as their earlier vision of my infancy. It can be ludicrously simple; it can happen through the impulsive application of a tape measure. Suffice it to say there is no redress against it. For a prodigy, abnormality is licensed. Precocity is tolerable (even amusing, fascinating) because it will disappear: that is its meaning, its nature. But when it shows signs of prolonging itself; when development (their language, not mine: I have never developed) appears indefinite, or worse, infinite, it becomes threatening, a monstrosity.

Puberty (or rather the expectation of it) is the blank wall which demonstrates to me my latest cul-de-sac. I face it now: the point of *da capo*. Stripped and humbled, lawsuits round my head like a cloud of bees, the time arrives for me to return to an old beginning.

FOUR

The curtains at the french windows have not moved now for a long time. They have taken legal advice about me, I imagine. Who can they sue? The telephone is constantly in use; there is a bell at the outside corner of the house under the guttering from which tremors issue. When the time comes the windows will fly open like the doors of a cuckoo clock, and they will march out shoulder to shoulder. Caitlin will turn back after a few steps and shut the windows; for she cannot bear that any dust should settle on her dining-room suite, especially after the maid has just polished and lavender-waxed it. But they will arrive together at the edge of my sandpit; she will give a little run to catch up, her tweed skirt brushing noisily against her thick stockings, her sensible shoes crushing the spring grass.

The forsythia is out. The scent of hyacinths drifts towards me from the sunny wall. I reach out. I can touch the air; it is thick with reality, heaving in waves against my retina, as I stretch forth my hand. Yet its particularity, its here and now, I know to be an illusion. It is shot through with lack of time; just as the garden, despite the infinite variation of its shades of green, is shot through by the spectrum; the bars of its visible cage. Was it the empiricist, Locke, who maintained that a trumpet sounded red to a man blind from birth? I shall be the blind man here. I shall fix it all arbitrarily – a stuck motor horn in a scarlet blare. In my pocket, against the thigh of my grey worsted shorts, I can feel the lump of my mother-of-pearl handled, Sheffield-steel penknife.

A flurry of stabs, and I shall be there. I shall be like a lark, trapped for hours in an empty theatre; having endlessly banged against flats painted with *trompe l'oeil* fruit trees. Interminably buffeted against rafters camouflaged with gilded clouds, it flies in desperation to the top of the auditorium and finds there, high up in the roof, a tiny chink. Fluttering, it squeezes through; instantly it corkscrews upwards, tumbling at last in a medium as real as itself.

The thought, of course, is pure melodrama, as grotesquely undermotivated as one of Roma's romantic operas. Reality does not yield so easily to ambition. The horn sounds again, insistent. Otto waits, an old man with a new limousine. Adam is paradised yet again, beating the bounds of his hedges and fences, his head bobbing up and down as he goes, a target, absurdly visible to the wilderness. Were there anyone out there so simple to imagine as a man, a sympathetic brother, squinting through his telescopic sight, inhuman mercy in his heart!

BAGLEY'S PROGRESS

Just as I knew he would, my father insisted on our sitting in the front row. Loudly, he suggested to everyone where and how they should make a space for us, policing their discomfort with a variety of hand signals.

The tent was grimy, great yellow streaks running down its sides. The ring was still visibly a field; thistles, ineffectually trodden down, reared up at a forty-five degree angle from the sawdust. I hunched up next to my mother, eyeing the only thing of interest to me: the rusty-blue car with yellow wing-flashes which, the poster had said, was going to loop the loop.

A girl with a forced smile on her face came into the ring and led round some horses. As she leapt on its back, one of them opened the corolla of its anus, turning inside out the purse of dark-brown velvet, and lopped out a quantity of khaki excrement, which landed directly in front of us and began to steam into the audience in dank, drifting clouds. I could see the skin stretched taut round her mouth as she fled past, her arms flung wide. The gesture seemed to have been learnt by everyone and they all persisted in performing it, even if they were just crossing the ring, or picking up a drum – they ran, in a curious skipping fashion, usually backwards, and flung their arms wide.

The ringmaster did it, after announcing that the car would not be going tonight, 'owing to a technical fault'.

But the clowns came, and everyone immediately started to laugh. There were two of them: the nasty-looking one with the spangles who played an out-of-tune saxophone, and an old man with a melancholy bush of grey hair under his bowler, a red nose, and baggy trousers, who kept looking over to where we were sitting as if he had seen something. After the other one had gone off, he bounded over and stood close to us on the wooden section of the ring, stretching his braces and letting them smack against his shirtfront. He leered down at us, his chin thrust out. Then he beckoned.

Instantly my father took my wrist and hauled me to my feet. Go on boy, he said in my ear, and offered me to the clown. Harold, my mother started to say, but the clown had me by the wrist now. I stared at his face. It was a mass of seams and wrinkles. The smile was painted on the upper lip. In reality he was scowling when you got up close, and he kept banging a roll of newspaper impatiently against his thigh. He dragged me running across to the centre of the arena.

'What's yer nairm mairt,' he said in a broad Yorkshire accent.

'Harolbagley,' I said all in a rush.

'Can yer do a rorl,' he asked. 'Yer knor, orva?'

I nodded, turning back to where my family was sitting. They seemed very far away.

'Reet!' shouted the clown. 'Get *goor*win' then!' and brought his tightly-rolled newspaper down on my head with a tremendous thwack.

I tried to look towards the huddle of my parents, as the lights screwed round.

'Yah!' I heard him shout from somewhere above me. '*Yah!*' as I stuck, buttocks in the air, in the last part of the forward roll. 'YAH!' as the newspaper came down on my upturned end with another dense report.

When I looked up at him again, he was still making the gesture, arms flung wide, head back, one long shoe out in front of the other.

It was the first time that I had been touched by anyone other than my family. Afterwards I looked for a long time in the wardrobe mirror at my hands and feet. I felt different. But no one seemed to treat me differently, and gradually I forgot about it. My mother called me Harold, my father Boy, or Harrymylad, my little brother Hawa', the teachers Bagley: all this added up to Harold Bagley, embryo of dignity and civic virtue.

It was inevitable that I should defend the creature whose Wagon Wheel was being eaten by Batho. Convention demanded that I issue the challenge.

'All right, Batho,' I bawled, 'I'm going to fucking *kill* you!'

Batho was built like a bosun. He looked at me through slit eyes.

'Afterwards,' he said through pursed lips, and the cry was taken up along the ranks that flowed towards the door in the corner of the playground. 'Afterwards, yeah, *after*wards . . . '

At the door, the crowd waited like so many flunkies. Convention also demanded that we jostle, Batho and I, all the way down the half-lit, stinking corridor. I put a lot into that jostling. Batho was imperturbable, the ringworm shining like a tonsure in his bullet crown.

Afterwards arrived and we streamed out to the field behind the school. My aides walked all around me, offering tactical advice of a conflicting nature. I heard my name on the lips of others. Hubbub told me I was a hero.

'Who is it?'

'Harold Bagley and Fat Batho.'

'Oh, Bagley'll *kill* him . . . '

We swung over the stone wall, scorning the stile, and stood at either end of the corridor of spectators. I was Harold Bagley and I was going to kill Batho. He stood and waited for me. I was inclined to talk. The crowd were quick to take this for a coward's tactic. They began to catcall.

'Come on, Batho!'

'Come on, Baggy!'

What did they call me? Come on, *what*? My chest, but a moment before as full as a robin's, began to deflate. The word pricked me, as surely as if I had been stabbed by my mother's emerald hatpin. I shrank inside my clothing, my staring face hot and stubborn.

Somebody laughed.

A shove from behind rocked my head back. Batho advanced in jerks, propelled in turn by different sections of the crowd. I windmilled obligingly. Mere Baggy-stuff: his fist connected crisply with the centre of my face. The contours of my mouth had disappeared: it was wet, and full of alien bits. As they stared down at me, as if from the parapet of a well, I heard a voice of bottomless disgust say:

'Christ, you're no *use*, Baggy!'

I dragged home. No use. I was Baggy, a nonsense on two legs. I couldn't be taken seriously any more.

It was hardly a surprise when my little brother ran out of the house to greet me in his two-tone siren:

'Bag . . . geee . . . bag . . . geee . . . '

I despised him in almost every way, but the fact was that no one thought of calling him that, even though we shared the same surname. My very efforts to riposte stuck in my throat: somehow it fitted me, and not him. What was it about *me* that I could change? It wasn't just the incident, which passed from legend into oblivion, but the name – the name went on, no matter what new friends I acquired, and I deliberately, doggedly did the rounds. Somehow those two hateful syllables had tipped the world on its axis.

The auditorium was dark. I could scarcely make out the edge of the stage, but everywhere the creak of chairs, the random, but ceaseless, low coughing, spoke of the hot concentrated presence of fifty or sixty people. The opening had gone well. My inky cloak. I was standing in the wings looking for my mother's hat. I didn't know whether I was good or not, but everyone said I was:

'Harold, you were marvellous.'

'Thank you . . . thank you . . . '

'Depending on you, Bagley,' said the headmaster.

I knew that Clare was somewhere in the audience with her contemptuous friend Gail. Pale Clare, leader of the intellectual coterie, with whom I was in love. Beside me, smoking a cigarette, stood the Ghost, Robinson, the tallest boy in the school. We had just careered off together and we were listening for Johnson, Rice, and Canber to come bumping their way off.

—Something is rotten in the state of Denmark.

—Heaven will direct it.

—Nay let's follow him.

Robinson swept aside the curtain and the glare fell upon him. He stalked away. I heard the shuffling of others behind me and a giggle. For a moment something shot into the back of my mind, but then I too had launched into the glare and the automatic spring in my knees was released, sending me gliding after him to halt near the rat-hole centrestage, my arm upraised.

—Whither wilt thou lead me? Speak; I'll go no further . . .

Robinson was nearly in the audience. I was late. We had worked hard on this routine, and its success depended on my keeping the right distance from him. My throat was dry. I flicked my glove.

—Mark me.

—I will.

Robinson came towards me, circled noisily behind, and mounted his pedestal upstage. He lifted his heavy sleeves and warbled,

> — . . . My hour is almost come
> When I to sulphurous and tormenting flames
> Must render up myself . . .

I knelt, quickly in with my eager

—Alas, poor *ghost!*

After that, I could relax. It was a matter of remaining still, mouth wide open, eyes staring pebble-like, while he did the fretful porpentine. His big moment. My mind wandered as his mouth mumbled on through the long speech. I listened to the scrape of chairs. Out of the corner of my eye, I could see the salmon costume of the headmaster's wife in the front row.

Robinson was slow.

—Revenge his foul . . . and most . . . un . . . nat . . . ural . . .

It was his build-up.

—MURRRRRRRRR . . . DERRRRRRRR . . . I was quickly in again.

—*Mur*der?

But Robinson was running down like a record, his voice getting deeper and deeper. He rambled and bumbled his way through a labyrinth of repetitions:

—Murder m*ooo*st foul as in the best it is.

But this . . .

Yes?

 . . . m*oooooooooooo*st foul . . .

I shifted position, my jaws aching. What was the matter with him tonight? I could hardly believe the time this was taking.

Yes? Yes?

 . . . straaaaange and un–

His 'natural' was drowned as I cut in:
  —Haste me to know't, that I with wings as swift
  As meditation or the thoughts of . . .
Remember Clare, remember Ophelia. I turned my head towards
the audience for the emphasis.

                . . . *love*
  May sweep to my . . . REVENGE . . .
He began again, and I could hardly believe the sickly smile
that came over his face as he turned towards me. My throat
constricted.
  —Now, *BAGGY*, hear . . .
It was unbelievable. He hadn't said *that*. He couldn't have. The
qualm rose like a tide up my backbone. The smile. His voice
droned on, jambangling through the speech, far far away. There
was a noise in my ears like the sea pounding on the strand. It was
difficult to breathe. The sickly smile came creeping back again. I
croaked:
  —O my prophetic soul
  My *uncle*!
Robinson's shoulders were rippling, and his voice yodelled with
suppressed laughter as he went on with the speech. I went hot and
cold. It *couldn't* have been. I must have been hearing things. I tried
to pull myself together, to move away from him and echo to the
audience, who fortunately didn't seem to have noticed anything,
the frustration of his
   . . . won to his most shameful lust
  The will of my most *seeming* queen . . .
I smacked fist into palm, as I had done at rehearsal. The pause
was interminable. I turned to the audience, and then back to
Robinson, who gasped it out, loud and clear, so that it fell like a
stone.
  —Oh . . . oh . . . *BAGGY*: . . . what a falling off was there!
The audience tittered. My face burnt fiery under my make-up
and the sweat sprang into my palms. The headmaster's mouth was
beginning to open, as I made my way down to the lights and stood
looking out into the auditorium. Robinson started to struggle
through his next enormous speech in a monotone. I looked out over
the heads of the front rows. My voice was tiny, but a hush fell

immediately, and Robinson behind me tailed off as he realised I was talking:

'Mum . . . Dad . . . Sir . . . I just can't . . . Sorry, Mum . . . Dad . . . '

The headmaster rose to his feet and stood in front of me.

'Come on, boy,' he hissed, 'what's the matter with you? Come on: "O all you host of heaven . . . " Come on Bagley, man, what *is* the matter?'

He clicked his fingers to the wings.

'Prompt, prompt . . . '

I stood with bowed head, as the people began to get up and mill round. Someone touched me on the arm. The lights went up, and everyone was pushing back their chairs. My mother appeared, dabbing her eyes, threading through the crowd. The headmaster jumped on to the stage and stood beside me. All the way through his speech, she stared up at me and shook her head, while my brother plucked at the knee of my black tights until it hung down like an empty dropsy.

I was glad to retreat into my room and concentrate on my examinations. I took up the cello, sneaking out of the house after dark for lessons. My library books were changed by other people. I never saw Clare or any of my former friends. My brother was now fully preoccupied with his sporting life and had turned into a simple-minded lout. Most of the time, we referred to each other as 'Him'. I took solitary walks across the field opposite our brick hut of a council house, pretending to be delighting in the observation of nature. In reality, I hated walking, particularly when my feet got wet in the morning dew.

Meanwhile my father had retired from the railway and we had less money than ever before. My mother came upstairs one evening and knocked, timidly, on my door.

'What d'you want?'

She sat on the bed.

'Well,' she said with a sigh, 'it's your father.'

'What's the matter with him?'

'Now that he's retired, you know, Harold, we haven't got a lot to live on . . . '

'But we've got his pension, haven't we?'

'You boys cost something to keep.'

'Well, why doesn't "He" take a paper round, or something?'

'Ronald? He's going to, but that won't bring in much, will it?'

'He can support himself.'

She shifted position.

'Anyway, he's young . . . It's not really him . . . '

'I suppose Father can get a temporary job of some description, gardening or something, can't he?'

She shook her head.

'Doctor's told him to have a good rest. Anyway, he's worked hard enough really.'

I turned back to my papers.

'It's no use looking at me. *I* can't do anything, I haven't the time. You know I'm working for these examinations.'

'Yes Harold, I know your brain work is very important, but I was wondering . . . '

'The answer is *no*.'

She came to the desk and touched the back of my head.

'I know you're a good boy really, Harold . . . '

I flailed and waved her away. Sordid woman. All her talk of 'brain work' and 'highly strung'. What I had to do was to get out, away from these ignorant pigs of people, their backbiting little world, their obsession with the trivial details of other people's lives, to the free air somewhere. Where people were good to each other and took each other at face value.

I went over to the mirror.

Face value, that was all I wanted to be taken at. I turned sideways. I was handsome enough. Soon I would be accomplished. That was my word:

'D'you know, that's Harold Bagley over there at the corner table?'

'Oh?'

'Yes . . . terribly accomplished.'

I passed my examinations and went to Oxford. The rooks in the trees, the towers, the talk of Michaelmas and Epiphany, delighted

me. Here at last was a world where I could flower and be myself. I
didn't have to hide. I didn't have to be shy here, because no one
knew me.

In the vacations I lived on potato crisps rather than go home. My
room in Woodstock Road was a spartan cell, whose only luxury was
its whitewood bookshelves, which I filled with second-hand
Victorian editions of poets and philosophers. I imitated the accents
of my tutor, cultivating in particular the way he nodded and said
'Yah!' four times in succession during the speech of others. I joined
a small chamber orchestra, which used to meet on Sunday afternoons at Gerald's garden flat in St Ebbe's. Gerald was a Balliol man
and all sorts of people 'dropped in' to play. Most of them seemed
accomplished. In the summer, with the windows open, the bees
humming in the jessamine, and everyone calling me Harold, it was
heaven.

It was here one Sunday I met Ingrid. She was tall and dark, the
daughter of a professor of German. We had a long conversation,
while I stared excitedly at her faint moustache, about how much we
hated our parents. I couldn't bear to tell her my father was a
railwayman, so I pretended he was an insurance clerk. That was
quite clever as it turned out, because she was rather left-wing and
insurance clerks were particularly hateable, whereas railwaymen
had a certain romanticism to them. Ingrid called me Harry. She was
studying sociology, and said that I was upwardly socially mobile,
whereas she was going to be downward as soon as she got the chance.

'I have the feeling,' I whispered, imitating her cool smile, 'that
our arcs are about to intersect.'

That evening I went back to her flat and we took off our clothes
and got into bed. It was a wild success. She shouted, in her breathy
way, 'Oh . . . oh *Harry*,' and I was thrilled. It was the first time for
both of us, but I pretended that social mobility had given me plenty
of experience at this kind of thing.

I was filled with a new energy. On Sunday I heard myself say,
casually, to the other members of the chamber group:

'Why don't we take it from bar sixty-four, where Gerald has the
semi-quaver – the F-sharp – shall we? After four then, two . . .
three . . . '

Throughout the session I could hear the buzz of Ingrid talking to her friend in the kitchen, punctuated occasionally, as we rested our instruments, by a 'Harry', or was it a 'Daddy'? What did it matter?

I began to drift round with Ingrid's friends. I found their generalizations easy to handle. Every time they started a sentence with 'most people', I pounced. One evening in the pub, she spent a lot of time leaning over the next table. Someone took her arm and whispered for a long time into her ear.

'Magdalen guy,' she said, finishing her Pernod in a single gulp. 'D'you know what he called you, Harry?'

She giggled.

'My abrasive philosopher-friend.'

One afternoon Ingrid asked me round to smoke some Lebanese black. She was lying back against my pillow, curling a strand of hair round her finger.

I looked at her.

'Come here,' I said suddenly.

'Well, my friends . . . '

I waved.

'Bring them too . . . '

'Oh Harry . . . do you know what to *do*?'

'No, but try telling me.'

'Have you got a stereo?'

'I can get one.'

'Get some coffee, and some nice little things to nibble.'

'OK.'

'Are you sure you can handle this? I mean, d'you want to? I'll come and help . . . '

'Absolutely. Just leave it to Harry.'

'OK . . . One thing though,' she kissed the tip of my nose, 'don't get too heavy?'

It was hard to borrow a stereo. In the end I got Gerald to lend me his, at the price of an invitation to the party. I scoured the town for health foods and bought lots of spinach quiche with oatmeal pastry. I arranged the papers on my desk carefully, so that my story about the existentialist who was decapitated by helicopter blades lay uppermost.

Gerald and I sat listening to Poulenc playing Satie. He was nervous.

'What's this stuff like?'

'Bit hard to describe,' I said carefully. 'People say such different things.'

'I mean, for you?'

'Oh, marvellous, frightfully good.'

'Better than, you know, drink?'

'*Drink*, good God Gerald, not in the same . . .'

Ingrid's knock let me off the hook. They filed in. There was a lot of repartee as they went up the stairs. I was crushed against the wall. It was a different crowd. The second to last one paused on the doorstep and stared at me with round eyes:

'University man, *hey*?'

I dashed upstairs. Gerald looked bewildered. Ingrid was bending over the stereo.

'What are all these *townies*?'

She looked up as the choric opening of 'You Can't Always Get What You Want' began to thrum out of the speakers.

'Like the man says,' she flipped her wrist. 'Come on, Harry, let's *dance*.'

Even Gerald covered his mouth with his hand, while my knees and arms rose in stiff, random succession.

Ingrid threw her arms round my neck.

'Harry,' she whispered, 'you are so *sweet*.'

I smiled across at Gerald while she hugged me.

Several people were kneeling together in the centre of the room, attending to the manufacture of some enormous-looking fishtail joints. The acrid smell of sulphur was followed by the scent of hashish. Someone closed the curtains and in the half-light I felt the paper tube slip into my hand. Ingrid smiled up at me from where I lay on the floor. As I sucked in, the glowing end, forming the centre of a cascade of ash and paper-fragments, leapt towards my lips, and my mouth filled with a cloud of smoke I didn't know what to do with. My cheeks out like a goldfish, I passed it to Gerald. He looked at me inquiringly. I nodded, closed my eyes, and sucked in. An impenetrable wall of smoke hit my lungs. Stifling the choking sensation, I held my breath. Gerald was still looking at me. I smiled at him, my mind suddenly in my ear. The room was filled with giggles. Everyone seemed to be giggling. I felt the irresistible desire too. Little bursts of speech dribbled delightfully from me and shouts of laughter went up all round. Gerald was looking pale and frightened. He got up and went to the bathroom. A long time seemed to have passed and I was astonished to find it was only five minutes. Everything seemed full of allegorical potential, every chance remark springboarded the company into sophisticated whirls of glee. Even Gerald had recovered. To everyone's delight, his laugh was hysterical, tragic, donkey-like.

'Go on, laugh *again*, Gerald!'

'Huh . . . huh . . . huh . . . huh . . . '

Ingrid smiled, her eyes wrinkling down into her cheeks, which were themselves wrinkling like sand through water. Smiling, smiling.

'Like a beach,' I said.

She nodded for a long time.

I was talking to my neighbour on the other side. His mouth was full of quiche and he swayed back and forth with his eyes shut.

I was saying, 'I mean, you have this proposition A, right?'

He swayed.

'Well, to justify believing in *that*, you have to have a further proposition, right, to the effect that it is overriding evidence for the truth of A, called B, right?'

He nodded.

I caught him under the elbow.

'Just keep still a moment. *Now*, to believe in *that* . . . '

I felt Ingrid shaking my arm on the other side.

'. . . you have to have this other proposition C, to the effect that it is overriding evidence for the truth of B, *right*?'

'Right.'

'And to believe in *that*, you have to have another, to believe in which you have to have another, and so on. I mean, just don't talk to me about Sufi, right?'

He opened his eyes.

'*Such* good pie,' he said.

I turned to see what Ingrid wanted, but she was up at my desk leafing through the papers. The needle was worming back and forth on the last grooves of a disc and the room had fallen quiet. I was half-struggling to my feet, when she sprang electrically away from the desk, holding an envelope at arm's length.

'I misread it,' she shouted, 'I misread it!'

Everyone looked up.

'Ha ha ha,' cackled Ingrid.

Prickles began to run up my neck. Something seemed to have come adrift here. I couldn't get my breath properly.

'What?' called out Gerald.

Ingrid squinted at the envelope again and looked over at me like a witch, her chin sticking right out.

'It's so funny,' she said, 'I thought it said Harold BAGGY . . . HAHAHAHAHAHAHAHAHAHA . . . '

'God, Baggy,' repeated someone.

'*Baggy*, that's good, Harold, eh?' said Gerald. He turned to the others. 'Suits him in a way.'

I couldn't believe my ears. How had this happened? I looked at Ingrid, who was bending towards me in a paroxysm, the wisps of blue-black hair over her ears trembling, like coiled springs, with her laughter. 'Oh God,' snorted her voice at last, '*Baggy* . . . Oh God . . . ' while her fingers pulled helplessly at an elastic band that held the envelope, stretching it and letting it crack again and again against the paper.

My suit was of flecked mauve tweed. I wore the waisted trousers on the hips, and, despite cleaning, the concertina marks which began at mid-shin were permanent. Every September I put it on and went in to see my colleagues. While the headmistress droned on about the trivialities of the coming year, I looked out of the window.

It was still there. It was always still there. Across the yard, scrawled diagonally in tarry strokes on the brick, was the legend:

FUCK OFF BAGGY

The odour of the staffroom – that fug of central heating, sweat, chalk dust, and tea dregs – had not been obliterated by the summer vacation and the recent efforts of the cleaners. Griffiths, the Welsh mathematics teacher, was always among the first to greet me in his loathsome Swansea vowels, 'Hullo Bagg*ee*, had a good holiday?'

'Hello Griff, just pottering about . . . And you? Go down to Bangor again this year?'

Howells, who referred to himself as the 'chemistry wallah', and his six-foot-four-inch wife, the art teacher, came stalking past on their way to the car. They lived in a rectory in Peckham and called each other Rat and Mole. The telephone engineer, who was having an affair with Mrs Howells, was called Badger.

'Hello Baggy!' they chorused, 'back again!'

Some of them went further. The games master called me Bag. And the R.E. teacher, a socialist from Ampleforth, called me Baggers.

It was all just like my suit: it was an open secret. From the day I walked into the Manor, I was Baggy Bagley, Remedial English and Drama, an uncomfortable, permanent fixture. In only my second week, a group of boys followed me home. I was forced to make a detour, while they kept half a street behind, cupping their hands rounds their mouths and whistling. Even when I got home, I thought I could hear them through the window, two or three streets away, faintly calling 'Bag . . . geeeeeee . . . ', and I ran into the bathroom and turned the taps full on to get rid of the sound.

But none of it mattered any more after the arrival of Auberon, even the scrawls in the toilets. It was indeed all just like my suit, just a garment I wore for the purpose of earning my money, and Auberon showed me that it didn't fit. When I looked at it like this, it even caused me a twinge of sour amusement.

When I met him, Auberon was standing in the door of the 'Non-Nisa' café in St George's Street. I sat down at one of the tables and ordered an expresso coffee and he sauntered inside. When he came out with the coffee, he goggled sideways at the books. Meanwhile I was goggling at the enormous gold buckles on his strapped, high-heel shoes. Under the straps, the skin of his pronounced ebony ankle had a sheen in the sunlight like a silk stocking.

He had two cups with him and sat down on the other side of the table.

'What arr you rea*din*'?' he asked.

I laughed nervously.

'Oh just bedtime stuff,' I said.

He picked up a copy of Aristotle's *Nichomachian Ethics* and looked at the spine. He made a face.

'Ay like rea*din*' ' he said, removing his shades.

He held up his hand.

'Lissen,' he said and began slowly to recite, "Do bee. Orr nodd do bee. Zatt iss zerr kawesha." You know what zat iss?'

I nodded.

'Say eet.'

'Shakespeare, Hamlet.' I said obediently.

'Shackspeer.'

I looked at the coffee. It was starting to wrinkle over.

'Do you normally come out and sit with the customers?' I asked.

Auberon threw back his head and shouted with laughter, showing me a semi-circle of brilliant white. He rocked forward on his chair, placing a pyramid of fingertips against the gold medallion that gleamed through his open shirtfront:

'You sink ay yam zee way*terr*?'

He was from the French-speaking Camerouns. He was going to study to be an architect. He had got off the boat with four pounds in his pocket, and made straight for Chelsea. Currently he was living with a hairdresser in Fulham, but William and he were getting on each other's nerves. Auberon couldn't bear his friends to smoke, and William smoked, clandestinely, at the salon. When I asked him his name, he took off his shades again and grinned. 'Ay yam Auberon, ze king of ze ferry.'

I laughed, 'And I am the Queen of Sheba.'

Quick as a flash, he extended his hand over the table and his deep brown eyes locked into mine. 'My d*eeeerrr*,' he purred. 'Ay yam ver . . . ray pleese to meet you.'

His voice, as he explained that his father had been a fan of Shackspeer, was beautiful. It was husky and had a little catch in it. The accent was an incorrigible patois of Fulham and Cameroun

French. I listened for that catch, as I plied him with questions. Why on earth hadn't he gone to Paris instead of London?

He whinnied. Then his face became very grave. 'Meesteck,' he said. 'Ay sord I *wass goin'* zerr.'

I took him back to my gloomy flat overlooking Vauxhall Bridge. He clapped his hands in excitement and nosed round everywhere. The rooms were almost bare. Eyes shining, he asked me for twenty pounds and disappeared. I saw him from the window springing through the traffic. Half a day had gone by before the doorbell rang. The man handed me a tiny mahogany table with the ticket still attached to the central leg.

Those were the last days of the summer term, and gradually he filled the flat with little things, ready for our life to begin. One evening I dragged myself upstairs to find the door already open. A hand shot out and pulled me inside. He was standing behind the door, heavily-perfumed, wearing a shirtwaister in orange cotton with patch-pockets and a half-full skirt. His feet were raked up almost vertically into a pair of tall green sandals and a matching handbag in green leather hung from the crook of his elbow. He shimmied. Under his long chestnut wig, he pouted, kissing me in the ear. 'Mm . . . shoogarr,' he said, 'ay yav sumsinn' forr you.'

Leading me by the hand, he swayed like a tightrope walker into the bedroom. Across the bed lay the bodice of dark blue jersey with its triangular hipster skirt, panelled in strips of blue and white cotton. My blonde wig crowned the mirror. My blue court shoes lay in their tissue-lined box.

Every evening for the rest of the term, after sleeping for an hour, I showered and put on my dress. We sat in the bow window watching the barges come and go on the Thames. At precisely ten minutes to six, Auberon tottered solemnly in on his green spikes, balancing the clinking tray with the ballerina on it.

We sipped Campari and Vermouth, talking until the lights came up on the Tate Gallery, while a wonderful aroma from the kitchen made itself felt. We talked about books, the UPC struggle in the Camerouns, the Germans, the French, and above all the cooking of chickens. Auberon knew fifty ways to cook a chicken and we planned to write a book together. He wanted to know everything that went on at school, and my satire, which tended to suggest that I was a dignified, slightly awesome figure, deeply respected by those for whom I showed my obvious contempt, came into its own, flowering to anticipate every whicker of his butterfly nostrils. We took photographs of each other and developed them in the bathroom. We redecorated the flat from top to bottom. I bought a fourposter with crimson curtains of fringed velvet, and in this coach-like space, while the muslin drapes swelled in the breeze from the river, we lay in state, Auberon keeping up a continuous patter of obscene French to accompany the roaming of his pale finger-tips.

Rome was our great adventure.

The Albergo Fiora on the Via Viminale was run by a cousin of Mario Sidoli from the Non-Nisa. The lady making out the *fiche* looked at my passport and screwed up her eyes.

'Signor . . . ?'

'Bagley.'

'Backlee. Number Seven.'

We did the Borghese on a Sunday, where Auberon insisted on our imitating, in front of two German coach-parties and their guides, the Apollo and Daphne of Bernini. We photographed each other on the Capitoline Hill and in the Baths of Caracalla. We walked arm in arm through the Vatican apartments and got the same crick in the neck. We bought new dresses and on our last night we were determined to wear them. The pensione was over a cinema and rather than trying to brave the Signóra who watched the door by day and night, we bought tickets and changed downstairs in the gents, planning to have supper and return to change before the programme finished. I explained to Auberon about Cinderella.

'Zenn we are two pompkeens!' he shouted, as we clattered out of the marble foyer and down the steps.

The *trattoria*, which we had picked out during the day, had cheerful tablecloths of red gingham and was rather out of the way. Our elation knew no bounds. The waiter was astonished at the amount of Frascati we were drinking. After a while, Auberon began to get silly. He made faces at me across the table, one of his most unamusing tricks. Then he picked up the menu and hid behind it, peeping round the side every two or three seconds and calling me by the name of a different item:

'Signorina *Melanzaane* . . . Signorina *Fettuciiine* . . . Signora *Zabagliooone* . . . '

He got on to this Zabaglione track and couldn't get off it. He seemed to think this was particularly witty, and began sounding the 'g':

'Signora . . . Signore . . . Zabag . . . ' he fumbled, feeling his way in his unerring sing-song towards a goal which, through all the mists of wine and distance, in all the gilded mirrors of the restaurant, I suddenly recognised, a split second before him, looming ahead.

He dropped the menu, thrust his chin across the table, and pointed at me, his face creased up in a demoniacal sneer.

'You!' he shouted. 'You Signore ZZZZZZZZZBAGGY . . . '

An accomplished face at the next table turned and clucked loudly.

'Yess you arr . . . ' hissed Auberon under his breath.

'All right,' I yelled, kicking back my chair and snatching up my bag. 'You can pay for this, you filthy black bitch!'

I attempted to sweep out. But Auberon was already limping at my side, fawning and doffing his wig in the fashion of an obsequious cotton-picker. Out of the corner of my eye, I saw the manager leave his post and start down the aisle behind us, followed by the waiter:

'Ma, signori . . . non hanno pagato!'

We reached the doorway at the same time as the three priests, each leaning at a severe angle and cramming his biretta to his forehead, struggled in out of the squall that was blowing in the street. For a moment, despite the flapping of our garments in the draught from the door, we formed a motionless kiosk of bodies some four feet in diameter. I stared down at the empty expanse of chequered tiles between us, as the diners all around, some still chewing or holding a limp napkin, began to scrape back their chairs and rise to their feet.

NADA

For two days and nights Angelines lay with her finger inside Concepción, waiting for my head to come. When it did, Angelines took me in the back to wash me off. Straightaway, Concepción shouted to know what I was. Angelines couldn't tell at first. Hadn't she driven herself nearly blind all these years, delivering other people's babies? But then . . . A girl, she shouted back.

Angelines told me this herself.

Concepción called me Maria, after her mother. The same afternoon she was out at the *lavadero*. Galicians are like that. They have to be, to live there. In Madrid, they have a saying about the climate: *nueve meses de invierno y tres meses de infierno*. Nine months of winter and three months of hell. But in Galicia, people just get on with it.

Everyone in La Vega knew the Puentes. It was a house of women. Concepción, Rosalia, Juana, Encarnación, Josefa, and Maria. Our father Jaime Salvador Puente inherited the smallholding, but the land was no good. He went south to Andalusia to get money. When I was four, news came to say he'd been killed in an accident at the mica mine. Concepción went into mourning for seven years. I can't remember anything of him, except the dim idea of someone playing a bagpipe at a *fiesta* in the plaza.

Francisco was away in the navy. Antonio went to be a *resinero* in the pine forests in Segovia. They sent us a little money sometimes, but I never knew either of them.

Ramon the eldest, named after our Grandfather, fell from the cliffs and was killed before I was born. He was Concepción's favourite.

We worked from morning till night. We did everything we could think of to survive. We shared the crops and ran the farm that way. Dôna Pilar was hard, but she was fair when there was a bad harvest.

Josefa and I, being the youngest, had the *recoveria*. We walked miles collecting those eggs. Then we put them in the plaza, ready for Cristobal's taxi to take them to El Ferrol in the morning.

One day we were bringing the eggs home, when we stopped to

pick some flowers on the cliff. While we were there, the Freire boys came from behind the eucalyptus trees. They started laughing and pulling Josefa about. They didn't see Petrolero, who was doing some work in the maize at the end of the terrace. Josefa whispered in my ear she wouldn't be long, I must stay there. Then she went off with the Freires behind the walls of the fort.

I cried for a bit, but then I forgot. When I looked up, Petrolero had worked his way right along. It was late and we had a long way to go to get to La Vega. I started crying again. When he heard me, Petrolero stopped work.

He came over to me.

'Weren't there two of you?' he asked. 'Where's your sister gone?'

I didn't want to tell him she'd gone with the boys, so I said I didn't know. He said she'd be back soon. He kept laughing to himself and showing the big gaps between his teeth. Then he sat down and took out his pipe. But he didn't light it. I wanted him to light it, but he just sat there with it in his hand, looking at me. I stood up and looked for Josefa, but I couldn't see her. I could hear them laughing somewhere up in the ruins. Petrolero's hand touched the back of my leg. I moved away an inch or two, pretending to look for Josefa, but his hand came back and pulled at my leg. He turned me round. His tongue was lying out on his bottom lip like a big slug. He pulled me close so that I couldn't get my breath. I could feel him fumbling. But then he stopped and snatched away his hand as if he'd been burnt. He growled something to himself. Then he came back and lifted up my skirt between his finger and thumb. He gazed at me and poked. He made me open my legs and crooked his finger underneath.

'But . . . what are you?' he said.

I looked away for Josefa, feeling the breeze between my legs and wondering what he was going to do next.

'What are you?' he said again. I whimpered. He shook me and made me look into his bloodshot eyes.

'You!' he said. 'You're a boy!'

Then he shouldered his tools and went away.

I don't know what happened after that. I remember looking at

myself and crying. Then Josefa was kneeling beside me and the
Freire brothers had gone.

'What's the matter, cry-baby?' she asked.

I told what Petrolero had said to me.

'Don't take any notice of him,' said Josefa, 'he's *loco*. But
Maria,' she took me by the hand, 'I want you to swear to me by the
Holy Virgin that you won't tell anything about today.'

I didn't think she meant her and the Freires, I thought she
meant Petrolero.

'I won't tell,' I said to myself, 'I won't tell anyone ever that I'm a
boy.'

Ramon was the name of my father's father. He was killed by the
FAI in the first days of the Civil War. They came into the village,
rounded up a few prominent people, and shot them. In the bundle
of things that came a few weeks after Father was killed at the mine,
was a tiny photo of Grandfather Ramon.

It was the first thing I stole. I kept it under the mattress.

The night after Petrolero had said that, I dreamt we were on a
pilgrimage up El Chamorro to the shrine of the Virgin. Petrolero
came from the top of the hill. He stood in our way. Then he took
out a *chorizo* and pointed it at me:

'This one is a boy!' he shouted.

I ran to him and struck at it. The skin broke open and thousands
of tiny photographs scattered on the ground. Before I could collect
them up, they winnowed off the side of the hill, floating on air
currents, down to the sea below. But Concepción and my sisters
and everyone else on the pilgrimage had picked one up and they
were all crying.

When I woke, Josefa and Encarnación were lying on either side
of me. I couldn't believe the dream wasn't true, for a long time. I
made sure the photograph was still under the mattress. But I
couldn't get back to sleep, I was so restless. I wanted to see
properly what they had down there, so I gradually worked up their
nightdresses and levered their legs apart. Encarnación kept rolling
over, so I couldn't see very well. But Josefa was very obliging and
lay snoring with her legs wide open. I was just bending forward to

look, when she lashed out with her foot in her sleep and kicked me like a mule on the jaw. Next morning, everyone wanted to know where I'd got such a big purple bruise. After that, I gave up trying to find out from them.

Rosalia and Encarnación were in service at Pontedeume. When I was eight, they took me with them to start work there. We went through the big gate and behind the orange grove to the servants' door. They left me at the door and went inside. Encarnación said I must stay there and wait. I would get into trouble, she said, if I went into the house.

After they'd gone, I grew bored. I wanted to go in too. So I tiptoed through the door and into the rooms. Most of them had dust sheets over the furniture. After a while I came to a little back staircase and went down it. There was a man waiting at the bottom with a sack in his hand. It was dripping.

'What's that?' I said.

'Come and look,' he said.

I followed him down a corridor. As he walked, the sack made red spots on the floor. We came into a room, overlooking the court-yard. Racks of guns lined the walls. He opened the sack and tumbled a heap of fur and feathers on to the table. I exclaimed and jumped back.

'That's just like a girl,' he said as if speaking to someone else. Then he took one of the guns and started cleaning it with a rag from the bench. He broke the gun and looked at me down one of the barrels so that I could see his eye.

'You must never point a gun at anyone,' he said, 'whether it's loaded or not.'

'Then you mustn't point that one at me,' I said.

He looked at me sharply and asked who my father was. When I told him, he said that I was a very forward little girl and I would do well to watch my manners. The explanation was that he was just showing me, so that I would know another time.

A bell rang and he jumped up and swore. In the courtyard was an old lady with a veil walking up and down. I saw him go out and talk to her, nodding all the time. I asked him who it was.

'The grandest lady in the world,' he said, smiling and trying to pinch my cheek.

He went back to cleaning his gun and asked me my name. He repeated it several times.

'Well Maria,' he said, jumping up, 'I want to show you something. I want you to go and stand in the middle of the courtyard by the fountain and look up.'

When I didn't move, he laughed and said he wasn't going to hurt me.

I stood by the fountain looking up at the windows and the balcony. Nothing happened. In the end, I went back and found him on his knees under the table. He came out and waved me back:

'Go! Go!' he shouted, cursing. 'Go back!'

Nothing happened again. But then there was a hiss and the fountain bubbled and spurted all over me. Then it died away. I could hear him screeching with laughter behind the window.

'I'm soaked,' I told him.

Tears were running down his cheeks.

'You did it,' I said.

He spread his hands.

'I . . . ' he said. 'How could I?'

In the end he calmed down, giving out little bursts of laughter and rubbing his knuckle in his eye. Then he told me to look out of the window. I saw him reach down. Then the fountain spurted and died away.

'But what about the town water supply?' I asked.

'The . . . what?'

He looked as if he'd eaten something bad. Then he threw back his head and tried to pretend he was laughing again.

I repeated the question. He looked sick, smiling and shaking his head.

'That doesn't matter here,' he said angrily. 'This . . . is Pontedeume.' He waved his arm.

'That is where you are wrong,' said a voice behind us.

The lady had been standing outside the door and had heard every word.

'The child is correct, Diaz,' she said. 'All of Spain is thirsty and *you* are playing with a fountain.'

He muttered odds and ends of things:

'. . . thousand regrets . . . didn't mean . . . showing the girl . . . didn't think . . . '

'Never mind all that, Diaz,' said the lady. 'Have you saddled the horses?'

She turned to me.

'And who are you, child?' she asked.

'Oh Dôna Pilar,' shouted Diaz, 'she's the washerwoman Puente's daughter.'

'Diaz,' said the lady, 'I didn't ask you for your opinion.'

'Maria Lucia Puente if you please, Dôna Pilar,' I said.

Diaz was stuttering and pressing down on my shoulders with all his weight.

'Leave the child alone,' said Dôna Pilar.

' . . . thousand apologies . . . thought the girl should show respect . . . didn't think . . . '

'Come with me, Maria,' said Dôna Pilar.

She took me through the house, asking about my family. We came to one of the landings overlooking the park. There was an ottoman under the windowsill. She lifted up the lid and took out a piece of white lace.

'Here Maria,' said Dôna Pilar, 'this is for your first communion dress. Now run along and help your sisters and don't go bothering Señor Diaz any more.'

I spent a long time thinking how to get my own back on Diaz for that trick with the fountain. He was always teasing me and making remarks because I was a girl. To distract him, I started telling tall stories about my brothers Francisco and Antonio. They always resulted in Diaz reminiscing about his army days. One morning I really didn't have any ideas left, so I started talking about my 'other brother'.

'I didn't know you had another brother,' said Diaz.

'Yes,' I said, 'he's . . . '

'He's what?' said Diaz.

'He's my twin,' I said suddenly.

'What's his name?' said Diaz, looking at me closely.

'Ramon,' I said.

'I can ask your sister,' he warned me.

I tossed my head.

'I don't care,' I said. 'Go ahead.'

I was astonished when he came back and started asking me questions about Ramon. I asked him what Rosalia had said. She'd been rushing by with some towels for Dôna Pilar's bath and had nodded.

'Poor Ramon,' I said, 'he's at death's door.'

'That's what your other sister said,' said Diaz.

I was even more astonished.

' "We *had* a brother called Ramon," she said,' Diaz replied, 'and looked so sad I thought she was going to cry.'

'Poor Ramon,' I said. 'He's so sick.'

The next day he came with 'something for Ramon'. I opened it on the way home. It was a little brass cannon that fired matchsticks. The next day: was Ramon any better? did he like his present?

After a day or so, I was bored with this. What else could I do with Ramon? I was just on the verge of letting him die, when I happened upon a little white sailor suit in the washing Encarnación had brought home to do. While I was waiting for it to be washed, I told Diaz that Ramon was getting better. Diaz began to get excited. I told him that perhaps Ramon would be able to come to Pontedeume.

'He can come shooting with me,' said Diaz. 'I'll soon make a little man of him.'

Eventually, after a lot of prompting from me, the sailor suit was washed. As soon as we got to Pontedeume, I took it from the pile which Encarnación had dumped in the kitchen and slipped out into the garden. I hid my dress under a bush.

When I came out, I saw Diaz talking to one of the gardeners. He stared at me, and then waved.

After they had finished their business, he came towards me up the path.

He opened his arms.

'Maria,' he said, 'what is this? Where have you got this new little boy's suit from?'

'Maria has told me many things about you, Señor Diaz,' I said, holding out my hand. 'I'm very pleased to meet you at last.'

He stopped in his tracks. Then he stepped on to the lawn and circled round me.

'Nooo,' he cried, 'I don't believe it!'

'I thank you for the present,' I said, still holding out my hand.

He took it, limply.

'Holy Mother of God, is it Ramon?'

I nodded.

'I don't believe it,' he said, laughing and shaking his head. 'You are so alike. But where is your sister?'

'Poor Maria,' I said. 'She's caught what I had.'

'Oh, she'll survive,' he said, putting his arm round me. 'But what's this, Ramon?'

He pinched the material of the suit.

'The army's the place for you, not this rabble of cowards.'

The following day, we went out shooting with the dogs. I was surprised to see the changes in him. He didn't interrupt me every time I spoke. He didn't tease me. He didn't pinch my cheek and chuck me under the chin with a sickly grin on his face. He didn't contradict me, though I said many of the same things.

Instead, he was serious. He strode out in front. He cursed all the time. He spoke as if he were thinking aloud. He taught me to sing the Madelon:

El Commandante Franco es un gran militar
que aplazo su boda para ir a luchar

He repeated El Caudillo's ten commandments after which he drew himself up to his full height and told me that he was Sergeant Diaz of the Legion.

We sat down, overlooking the sea.

'I like you, Ramon,' he said. 'You'll grow into a fine man. *Chiquillo*, I'm going to tell you something that has never passed my lips before. I'm a *gallego* and an old soldier and there's nothing I'm frightened of. Nothing in the world. Bullets, cannon fire, I've seen it all . . . Nothing, except one thing. You know what that is?'

I shook my head. I couldn't imagine.

'I'll tell you,' he said. 'When we were at the seige of Mellila, we sent the *regulares* up the western approaches. *Moros*, most of them, good soldiers too. They never washed, but they always kept their rifles spotless. It didn't do any good against Abdel Krim. They only had out of date Mausers and a few handfuls of the wrong ammunition. Poor devils. We pushed up behind them, just in time to meet the first survivor coming over the sand . . . What a sight they were! The first man I met was naked and burnt; he had a great wound between his legs. Before he died, he told me the Moroccan women had been hunting them down on foot and castrating them . . . '

'What's castration?' I asked.

He put his hand down between my legs and held me. Then he drew the imaginary knife across.

'Zeep,' he said, 'Mother of God, those women . . . I dream about them waiting for me to slow down and stumble and fall in the sand, waiting like vultures, their big knives flashing . . . '

He laughed bitterly, and clapped his hand on my shoulder.

' . . . and I wake up and my wife is kicking me.'

We got up. He sighed.

'You must grow up a tall *gallego*, Ramon my friend, and help El Caudillo fight these pigs that are trying to undermine Spain. These communist bastards don't know what some of us have been through for the *madre-patria*. Remember what he told the people of Mellila: "We are the Legion. We are prepared to die for you. Away with fear! The breasts of the Legion stand between you and the enemy. Long live Spain. Long live Mellila. Long live the Legion!" '

He stood to attention, staring out to sea, while I fingered my trousers, thinking of the wound and wondering what he had meant.

It was dusk when we got back to Pontedeume. I ran into the garden. I was worried, because I thought Rosalia and Encarnación must have been looking for me. The dress was still there. I could hear Diaz somewhere up by the house, shouting for me. I took off the sailor suit and was just putting my arms through the dress when I heard something. I turned. It was Diaz, standing in front of me.

'What's this?' he said.

I thought he would laugh. But he was terribly angry. He snatched up the sailor suit.

'You think you can make a fool of Diaz?' he yelled. 'You deceiving little bitch!'

I was frightened of the look in his eye.

'I'm cold,' I said shivering.

He snatched the dress from me.

'Take them off,' he said.

Slowly, I pushed my pants down to my ankles.

'Now,' said Diaz, 'you can walk home like that to show your shame, you little shameless bitch!'

Before I could do anything, Rosalia, Encarnación and Dôna Pilar suddenly appeared.

Diaz stood as still as a statue, clutching the sailor suit and the dress.

There was a lot of confusion. The women hustled me off and spent a long time questioning me. Did he put his hand there? What was I doing with my clothes off? I shook my head. I tried to explain that I had stolen the sailor suit and dressed up in it as a joke. But Rosalia and Encarnación were crying and Dôna Pilar was trying to make the telephone work.

When we were going through the garden, we saw Diaz walking with two men holding his arms on either side. I wanted to run after him and say it was all my fault, but all I could do was burst out crying.

'Poor Maria,' said Dôna Pilar as we reached the gate. 'Holy Mother of God, it is a miracle no less that we came by as we did. And to think,' she said putting her arms round me, 'every day she'd been in that gun room with him. He could have done anything.'

A few weeks later, Concepción got a letter from Dônar Pilar asking if she would permit her daughter Maria to go, at her expense, to the *Escuela de Sagrada Corazón* in El Ferrol.

*

Dolores Sepúlveda was my schoolfriend. Her family was poor like mine, but her uncle was the *Cácique* of Villa Real. He wanted her to marry well, so he sent her to school in El Ferrol.

Dolores lived in El Hoyo, a *pueblo* on the La Vega side. In the mornings we met at the fork on the cliff road and walked the last three miles into El Ferrol together. She was not very clever and I did most of her schoolwork in disguised handwriting, but Dolores was gay and always ready to have some fun.

One morning we were coming into El Ferrol as usual when we saw something flashing in the roadway. It was a pair of spectacles. Neither of us had ever seen them before, except on Sister Teresa. Dolores put them on.

'Ay!' she said. 'It's all blurred.'

'But they suit you, Dolores,' I said, 'I think you should wear them. I dare you.'

We pushed open the door of the classroom and I guided Dolores like a sleep-walker to her place. There was a lot of giggling. Sister Teresa held up her hand.

'Hush children. It is wrong to laugh at the misfortune of another.'

She guided Dolores up to her desk.

'But Dolores Sepúlveda, what is the matter that you should be wearing these?'

'Please Sister Teresa,' said Dolores, 'Don Claudio the *practicante* at El Hoyo says I must have them or I will go blind.'

Sister Teresa took off her own spectacles and asked to see them.

'My poor child,' she cried, handing them back, 'you must be almost blind already.'

She tapped on her desk.

'Children, children,' she said in her voice of concern, 'that is enough. Tonight, before we go to sleep, we must all say a prayer for Dolores and her poor eyes; I know myself what it is to have poor sight.'

Isabel Gamez nudged me.

'That's why no man would ever look at her,' she whispered.

After that Dolores had to put on her spectacles every day before coming into class. But a week later she lost them. Sister Teresa was most concerned. In fact Dolores' eyes were so bad that I had to thread her needle for her in the afternoon class and they didn't get back to normal for a whole day. When Sister Teresa realised that she'd been deceived, Dolores got into a lot of trouble. She had to go and see the headmaster, Don Miguel Coimbras. He was a priest with a violent temper, who frightened Dolores stiff.

But Dolores didn't mind all the extra rosaries, because it was my turn now.

For ages we didn't know what to do. But one morning, we came into school late and the boys were just going into their entrance. The school had been converted from a private house and had two entrances: the side one for girls and the main one for boys.

'I know what,' said Dolores, as we watched them filing in, 'I dare you to stand in front of the school there for five minutes.'

'That's too easy, Dolores,' I said.

'All right,' said Dolores, 'I dare you to go inside for five minutes.'

We discussed how I could do this without being noticed and decided that I would have a better chance if I wore boy's clothing. So over the next few days, Dolores brought an article of her brothers' clothing every morning. We hid them behind the door to the girls' entrance. When the morning came, I hid my own dress in the entry. The children were all inside the building chanting and Dolores couldn't stop giggling. When I stepped out into the light, I found it difficult to walk because her brother's shoes were too large. The trousers were supposed to be short, but they came down to my calves; and the jacket sleeves hung over at the ends and had to be tucked under.

On the top step I turned and waved to Dolores, wishing I was her. Then I pushed in through the door and shuffled down the hall.

On the wall was a board with the names of the old boys of the school who had been killed in the Moroccan campaign and the Civil War. On the other wall was a large picture of El Caudillo and underneath it the words

Be zealous ever of your reputation as a gentleman, purified as it were in a crucible.

I shuffled down the hall to the end. There were shouts and yells and a hissing sound. On the floor as I turned the corner were puddles of water and several heaps of clothes. The corridor was full of steam. In the steam I could see an open doorway, and through the doorway, where the steam was most dense, a group of naked shapes were sliding and skidding everywhere. Fragments of soap came flying through the doorway. I heard the swish of a cassock and a huge shape darted past me.

'*Coimbras!*' shouted someone.

'You people deserve *this* . . . ' I heard him say through his teeth. His arms flailed, smacking everywhere at once. One boy went down in the soapy gutter. 'All of you, Manuel Andrade, Inglesias, Canovas, Rivera and the rest of you, report to my office when you are dry.'

He paused in the doorway.

'Have you not been in the shower?'

'No, Don Miguel,' I said.

'New boy?'

'Yes, Don Miguel.'

'Name?'

'Ramon Carlos Puente, Don Miguel.'

He turned as the others began to troop out of the shower behind him.

'Come along, come along . . . Manuel Andrade, switch on the water again for Puente here, hurry!'

The showers hissed again.

'Come along . . . what are you waiting for?' he said briskly. 'Into the shower with you.'

They were staring at me. I started to lift my shirt over my head. It stuck.

'Give him a hand one of you,' I heard him say. Hands were pulling at me. My fingers fumbled with my trouser buttons, trying to undo them the wrong way round until I realised. Crimson rose to my face.

At last I was standing naked in front of them. I could feel their eyes on me. Someone giggled. I looked away waiting for the explosion.

'Well,' said Coimbras, 'what are you waiting for now?'

Talking beneath his breath about precious water, he pushed me into the steam.

'Don't forget to switch it off when he's finished,' he said to Andrade, cuffing him on the side of the head.

Outside the door they were fighting again. I stood in the steam until one of them came and switched off the shower.

By the time the steam had cleared, the hall was empty. I put on my clothes again and shuffled out.

'You've been in there almost an hour, Maria,' said Dolores running across the road to meet me. 'What happened?'

Even as I started to tell her and her face broke into a smile and she clapped her hands with delight, I realised there were some things I couldn't ever tell Dolores.

Concepción had sewn on Dôna Pilar's piece of lace and everything was ready. The service was to be held in the Ecclesia de Sagrada Trinitá in La Vega. On the day before, Sister Teresa had rehearsed us. The girls took the left side and the boys the right. At a prearranged signal from her, we were to get up from our seats in the first rows and file in an orderly fashion up to the rail. When the priest came to the person kneeling on our left, we should cup our hands ready to receive the sacrament.

As soon as we sat down, Dolores groaned.

'Maria,' she hissed, 'look who it is.'

Coimbras was gazing along the rows of intending communicants. His eyes rested on me for a moment, then passed on. Almost immediately, they stopped and swivelled back.

Once or twice during the service, I saw him gazing at me, an openly puzzled expression on his face.

Sister Teresa caught Isabel's eye. We filed up and knelt at the rail, the boys on our right. Impassively, the old Bishop of Ferrol came on, dropping the wafers into cupped hands. But when they were two heads away on my left, I saw Coimbras tiptoe behind him and whisper something in the Bishop's ear. He turned, startled, and asked a question. Coimbras shook his head. They came on. I cupped my hands. But they went to Dolores on my right. The next time they came round with the chalice, I put out my hands again. Again it was refused. As they passed, Coimbras whispered out of the corner of his mouth that he wanted to see me afterwards.

Everyone knew I'd been passed over. When they came out of the church they were all whispering. They stood around in groups on the other side of the plaza, the men out on the pavement and the women staring through the window of *El Portón*. The children ran in and out, between them.

We went back into church. Concepción was not as upset as I had thought she would be. The others kept worrying away at me, but she kept silent. Josefa in particular wanted to know what sin I'd committed that I should be refused my first communion.

'It must be something terrible,' she whispered.

Down the aisle came Coimbras and Sister Teresa. They sat down in the first row of chairs. Coimbras leaned on the back of the chair and stared at Concepción and myself. He drummed his fingers.

'I don't know how this set of circumstances has arisen,' he said at last, 'but I feel that someone owes me an explanation.'

Concepción was silent. Instead of bursting out indignantly, she looked down at the floor. She almost looked as if she knew and felt guilty.

'I'm waiting . . . ' said Coimbras.

I didn't understand. Concepción looked more and more ashamed every minute. In the end it was Rosalia who sat forward, thrusting her chin out, 'It's you Don Miguel, who owes us the explanation, causing us this shame in front of the whole village.'

'Be quiet, Rosalia!' said Concepción, but she spoke almost absent-mindedly, hanging her head again.

'I must confess, Don Miguel,' said Sister Teresa, 'I myself am somewhat puzzled by your action. Is there something I don't know about Maria-Lucia? She's been the best girl in my class, sure in her knowledge, sound in her catechism. It's true that she has raised the question of the sex of the Creator more than once . . . '

Concepción suddenly lifted her head. She was weeping. 'Yes yes I confess it,' she said. She clasped me to her. 'I was lax when she was born, Don Miguel . . . I didn't think it mattered . . . we were so poor when my Jaime went away . . . there was so much work to do, so many mouths to feed . . . '

She broke down.

'Carry on please, Señora,' said Coimbras. 'Enlighten us further, please do.'

'*I* know her name,' said Concepción, 'what did it matter to *me*? But I swear on the cross of our Lord Jesus, on the blood that pours from his Sacred Heart, I was not trying to be deceitful and wicked in doing this . . . '

She burst into sobs again.

'Somehow you have found me out, though I never told any-one . . .'

'Señora Puente,' said Sister Teresa, 'are you telling us that Maria was never baptised?'

Concepción nodded.

Coimbras was taken aback. But he remained horribly calm.

'Sister Teresa,' he said, 'would you mind, I would like to have a few words in private with Señora Puente and . . . Maria.'

Sister Teresa ushered out my sisters.

'Señora Puente,' he said, 'I'm glad for your sake that this has come out. It would have been quite meaningless to have administered the sacrament.' He smiled. 'I'm glad also that you have provided an explanation of the situation which will be believed by many people who hear it.'

Concepción smiled through her tears.

'But now that we are alone, I have to tell you that there is another reason why I did not administer the communion today. It is a much graver and more difficult matter. I hardly know how to say it. The fact is, Señora, that your daughter Maria here is not your daughter at all, but your son.'

Concepción began to babble.

'Don Miguel, what are you saying, she is Maria . . . my Maria, my youngest daughter . . . '

He looked at me.

'Admit it,' he shouted. 'Tell the truth!'

I ran to Concepción and hid my face in her skirts. Coimbras was breathing hard. I could hear Concepción murmuring and the echoes coming back from the empty church that Maria was a good girl.

'Is it possible, Señora Puente,' said Coimbras, 'is it possible that he had deceived you too and the whole of your family?'

'Don Miguel,' said Concepción, 'I have told you the truth. But now I don't understand your words. I don't know what you are saying to me?'

'The fact of the matter is,' said Coimbras, 'that he came into my side of the school not eighteen months ago. I myself *saw* him.'

'Look up, *chiquilla*,' said Concepción, shaking me. 'Now you must confess if you did this thing.'

'Yes,' I said, 'I did it because Dolores dared me to. All I did was dress up in her brother's clothes so that I could spend five minutes in the boys' side. That was the dare.'

'*Chiquilla*,' said Concepción indulgently, 'that was very naughty to deceive Don Miguel like that. Very naughty.'

Don Miguel looked at me and smiled thinly.

'The wolf,' he said, 'in sheep's clothing.'

He said he wanted to talk to Concepción alone.

When I got into the vestry, Sister Teresa was explaining to them how one couldn't have the holy sacrament before one was baptised.

Nearly an hour passed before Concepción came out. She was very pale. We all went across the plaza and when they saw us the people turned their backs.

Nobody spoke on the way home. Concepción was in a state of great uncertainty. She took me upstairs into the bedroom and shut the door. She looked at me.

'What is this Don Miguel is saying?' she said. 'You are my Maria, aren't you?'

I burst into tears.

'I don't know *what* I am,' I sobbed, rushing into her arms.

'There there, *chiquilla*,' said Concepción.

But after a minute or two, she sighed. 'I think it might be better if you didn't go in with Josefa and Encarnación tonight.'

Every Thursday evening, they met in the back room of El Porton to play a few hands of *tute*, drink a *copita*, and discuss the affairs of the *pueblo*. Don Ambrosio the *secretario*, Isidro the water-mayor, Don Manuel the *practicante*, and Eugenio the commander of the Civil Guard. It was not a coincidence that Don Miguel Coimbras liked to take his *moreno* there on Thursday evenings.

When Concepción and I got there, we had to wait in a cloud of cigar smoke while they discussed the dead pigs which Isidro had found in the irrigation channels. Nobody felt that swine fever was much of a serious thing, and in the end it was decided that they should bury the pigs and do nothing about it.

Concepción took me by the hand and we went up to their table.

'Yes,' said Don Ambrosio, 'what's the problem?'

'You asked us to come,' said Concepción.

'I?' said Ambrosio. 'Ah, but here is Don Miguel himself.'

Don Miguel sat down, nodding to everyone. Immediately Martin brought the black coffee and the sugar lumps flaming with a wavering blue flame in the saucer. They died down. One by one, he picked them up and dropped them in the cup while he told the story of my first communion, my appearance at the school.

He sighed. 'Señora Puente, I had hoped we could keep this between ourselves. But people are talking.'

'People are saying that Maria . . . ' said Don Ambrosio.

'Yes?' said Concepción.

' . . . is a freak,' said Don Ambrosio.

'Worse,' said Don Manuel.

Concepción looked from one to another.

'That she's a . . . ' said Ambrosio.

'A witch,' said Isidro.

'They're *loco*,' said Concepción.

'Perhaps,' said Don Miguel, 'but the question is what can we do to stop this talk.'

'We can act,' said Don Ambrosio.

'How?' said Isidro.

'We must call a meeting. We must confess the situation. We must say we . . . '

'I'm afraid the damage is already done,' said Don Miguel. 'You know what the *pueblo* are like once they get an idea in their heads.'

'We should send her away,' said Don Ambrosio. 'Don't you

have a *pariente* in Zaragoza?'

'There is my brother Fausto,' said Concepción, 'but Maria will not go away, while this body holds breath.'

'We understand how you feel,' said Don Ambrosio, 'but remember, Señora Puente, what people are saying. Do you want her to be a freak all her life. Unable to marry? Do you want to be called a witch too? That is what will happen. No one will look at you on the street. People will say you are *sinverguenza*. Do you want your house to be burnt down? But if she goes away, she can start a new life.'

'*She?*' said Isidro.

Then an argument started up as to whether I should go as a boy or a girl.

'She is my Maria,' said Concepción tearfully.

'But a man,' cried Isidro in his cups, 'a man is a leader. A man can do as he likes. *He* is the thing she should be. Besides, think of the money he will send back for you . . . '

'But a woman!' shouted Don Ambrosio, all red in the face, 'a woman is the finest thing on God's earth. She's put there for a man, but she is purer than him. Let her stay as she is . . . '

'Toss a coin,' grunted Eugenio, woken by all the shouting.

'It's not a matter of what's better,' said Don Manuel the *practicante*, 'but what's true. You're all talking as if there is some choice in the matter. But there isn't any.'

'Then she is my Maria,' said Concepción holding my hand tightly.

'Señora Puente,' said Coimbras at last, 'what concerns me here, as you know, is the question of the immortal soul. But, as St Paul says, the way to the soul is through the body. Now, it would be tantamount to sending him direct to the eternal flames if we were to leave his soul as it is, masquerading in a female form . . . '

Concepción looked at me doubtfully.

'What I'm prepared to do,' said Don Miguel, 'is baptise him. Since he was never baptised in the first place, it will be, to all intents and purposes, his first baptism, and his new life can begin the day afterwards.'

In the end, the men all agreed that I should be baptised.

'What shall he be called?' asked Ambrosio.

'What is the name of his paternal grandfather?' asked Coimbras.

'Why, the whole *comarca* knew Ramon Puente,' said Don Ambrosio.

'So be it,' said Coimbras.

'No no no no no,' shouted Concepción, banging on the table. 'This is my Maria.'

She dragged me out of the bar. All the way home, she muttered things to herself, hauling me through the potholes and the mud.

'A week later Rosalia and Encarnación came home early in the morning from Pontedeume. They brought a letter from Dôna Pilar. In it she explained that on account of 'the nature of my conduct' she had no choice but to have me withdrawn from the school. Moreover, she was reducing the number of domestic staff she employed and would regrettably no longer require the services of my sisters, though of course if either of them needed character references, they should not hesitate to . . . etc.

All day Concepción sat in the back of the house, wringing her hands.

'Ah, the shame,' she cried, 'the shame of it.'

Uncle Fausto's bar, the *Cocorico* in the Calle de Maria, was a Galician centre: everybody did their business there in Galician. Most of the clientele were men. Sometimes a few women came in on Saturday night for a *chato*, but they were mainly wives. The men stood or sat up at the bar, while the women sat in the corner. The *touristos* sat outside in the light.

Most afternoons Uncle Fausto was away at his cousin Claudio's garage, working on the cars. I did everything when he was away: waiting, washing, sweeping up. At first I made mistakes: I gave the wrong change. I didn't like Paco punching me in the arm. One night, in front of all Uncle Fausto's other friends, he got up on my back and made me gallop round the bar.

On Sundays, when the women came in, I couldn't get used to not going over and sitting amongst them. When they laughed and whispered and made eyes at one another, I strained to hear what they were saying.

But Uncle Fausto didn't like me talking to the women. I had to
stay over with the men. Whenever a woman came within earshot,
they all fell silent. Sometimes I would be caught out and go on
talking. There would be time enough for me to have a *novia*, said
Uncle Fausto, when I had some money. But he built me up to the
others. He said, jokingly, I was *sinverguenza* and he wouldn't trust
me with any women.

Work was good for me, he said, so I went to bed when the bar
closed and let up the canopy at six to give the *journaleros* their
morning *copita*.

It was different after Ladisláo came. He walked into the back of
the bar one morning and sat down. He was not a *touristo*. He was
not a *gallego* either. He was tall and dark and looked down his nose.
He carried a book or a newspaper to read.

He was *rico*. But he didn't seem to mind Uncle Fausto spitting on
the floor and muttering things about *los pudientes*.

'Are you a student?' I asked him.

He didn't look up from his book.

'Everyone in Spain,' he said, 'may be assumed to be a lawyer
until proved otherwise.'

'I'm not,' I said.

'No, Ramon, you are not. And neither am I.'

I asked how he knew my name. He tapped his ear and smiled
again.

After he'd been coming into the bar for a couple of weeks, he
asked me one afternoon if I'd like to go the football match. I told
him I had work.

'Pity,' said Ladisláo and shrugged. But then he nodded to
himself. 'Perhaps it's time to ask him all the same.'

Uncle Fausto was in a good mood. He and Claudio had sold a car
that afternoon. Ladisláo went up to them and sat at their table.
Uncle Fausto looked suspicious. I could see him looking Ladisláo
up and down. But Ladisláo leaned forward and said something,
and Uncle Fausto started nodding like a hen walking across a
stackyard. Ladisláo held up his thumb and jerked it over his
shoulder. Then they all got up and followed him to the door. I saw
them go over to an enormous green Packard parked across the

road. When they came back, I asked Ladisláo, 'What did you *say* to him?'

'Never mind that, Ramon,' he said. 'Your Uncle and I are men of the world. We understand each other. He's going to do a little work on my car for me. Now quick, put that towel down and let's be off.'

'Is this really yours?' I asked, running my hand along the wing of the Packard.

'Of course,' said Ladisláo. 'Now get in or we'll be late.'

I lay back in the deep brown leather seats and watched the sky going by.

'I've only ever been in Cristóbal's taxi before,' I told him, 'but that wasn't like this.'

He laughed and asked me why not.

'It runs on charcoal,' I said, 'and you have to get out on the hills and push.'

I liked the way Ladisláo never looked up from his book or paper. It was part of a game, I knew, so that Uncle Fausto wouldn't notice us talking. I wanted to ride in the Packard again, but Uncle wouldn't let me have any more time off. Then Ladisláo told me it had gone to the garage for some repairs.

One day I was taking Uncle a message to the garage, when I heard the sound of Ladisláo's horn in the street. He waved to me and swung the door open.

'I can't,' I told him, 'I have to go back.'

'I'll drive you,' he said. 'She's just having her first run and I'm anxious to try her out.'

'I don't want Uncle to see me,' I said, but I couldn't resist it.

'Shall I tell him?' said Ladisláo as we drove away.

I didn't know what to say.

'Don't look so worried,' he said. 'Oh look here, we're going past. Quick! down!'

His hand crooked over my collar bone and pushed me down into the scented leather.

'We're past now,' he said. 'It's all right.'

'I want to go back,' I said.

'Shan't be long,' said Ladisláo, 'I just want to show you my apartment. You do want to see it, don't you Ramon?'

As we walked up the stairs, he put his arm round my shoulder and looked down at me. He squeezed me.

'Ramon,' he said, smiling.

He showed me some photographs of the property his family used to have in Cuba. They'd been *rancheros* there at the time of the Spanish–American War. Now they were all lawyers and wanted Ladislão to be a lawyer too. We talked about La Vega and Concep-çión and my sisters.

He laughed and said I talked like a girl.

He sighed and walked over to the bed. He threw himself on it and lay with his hands clasped behind his head. He was restless and fidgety. He asked me if I would come and sit by him. Whenever I said anything, he giggled and chucked me under the chin or stroked my hair. I put down my glass and stood up.

'I must go,' I said.

'Ramon,' he said, holding out his hand, 'just lie down with me for a moment.'

I lay down. He propped himself on one elbow and put his tongue between his teeth while he fiddled with the waistband of my trousers. I stirred. But he pushed me down.

'No, lie back a moment. I only want a little . . . ' he murmured softly, 'I just want to . . . '

I lay watching his face. He breathed quickly, the tip of his tongue flicking over his lips, while he finished undoing the buttons.

I felt the air. He stared and moved back.

'Oh . . . ' he stammered. 'Oh, I . . . '

A blush spread into his face and neck.

'Please do up your things,' he said quickly, 'I'll drive you back straight away.'

He didn't speak until we were in the car again. His voice was different. Why was I pretending to be a boy? What was I doing? Did my uncle know? What was I going to do about it? Did I know it was wrong to deceive people? By the time we reached the side street and I got out of the car, he was quite angry.

Uncle Fausto was standing in the doorway when I got back. He looked me up and down.

'You take that message all right?' he asked.

'Not yet,' I said, trying to get by.

He spun me round.

'Ramon,' he said, 'I want you to keep away from that playboy. He's heading for trouble.'

For the next week, he found me so many tasks, I went to bed at night with my head and feet drumming. Ladislão didn't come. I looked for him, pretending to sweep outside.

On Friday afternoon, there were some *touristos* at the table outside who kept me running back and forth. Uncle Fausto was inside, drinking with Paco and Claudio. When I came in, they were laughing about something.

'Nobody shortchanges me and gets away with it,' said Uncle Fausto.

'*Hombre*,' said Paco, 'I'd like to have seen his face.'

'These *colonos*,' said Claudio, 'they think they can do anything.'

Uncle Fausto spat.

'Hey Ramon,' he said, 'the floor is dirty.' He picked up a newspaper that was lying on the table. 'Come over here and clean it.'

I bent down and started to tear off the front page. My eyes lit on some words in a column in the centre:

> . . . green Packard convertible, which
> had been cut into small sections,
> apparently with oxy-acetylene
> equipment, was found in a suburb
> of Zaragoza today

Uncle Fausto smiled at me, leant forward and poured himself another *copita*. 'Go on, *chiquillo*,' he said, 'what are you waiting for?'

I was glad to get my papers. After three years of Uncle Fausto, I was ready to leave Zaragoza. The medical examination was mainly concerned with my ears and feet. I had to put a tick or a cross by syphilis and hernia. The letter which arrived afterwards said that I should proceed to the barracks at Toledo for basic infantry training.

I was issued with a uniform, and shown where I was to sleep. It was a long dormitory. On one wall was a large photograph of El Caudillo. Underneath it were the words:

MAKE YOURSELF LOVED OF YOUR INFERIORS AND
DESIRED OF YOUR SUPERIORS

Underneath them, a group of people were having their heads banged against the wall by Corporal Canalejas. I handed him my papers and joined in the line.

'This is your *novatada*,' shouted Canalejas into my singing ears. 'We want to make sure you will be worthy of this glorious regiment.'

Then we were marched to a washroom, where the committee of four were sitting on the washbasins.

'Puente, Carlos Ramon,' said Canalejas. 'Strip him.'

He was holding a broom smeared with black.

I kicked and squirmed.

'Tell the coward to keep still,' said someone.

Canalejas peered.

'My God, that must be the smallest I've ever seen,' he said.

Someone whistled and a lot of jeering broke out.

'Shut up you lot,' said Canalejas. 'Hold him still. Big or small, the *hombre* must have his due.'

After that, I was known throughout the barracks as the man with the smallest in the world. Tiny Hose Vicente Suner, who came after me, was the man with the biggest.

On Saturday evening, after a week of tests and tortures, the committee of four met again. They told us it was time to test our *hombria*. It was time we made the acquaintance of Pepita, the soldier's friend.

A group of us were taken through the main gate of the barracks and over the bridge. The moon was shining. We entered a dark house and made our way to the first floor. All the girls came out of their rooms and hung over the balconies. The committee sat on the landing while the new recruits went in. Canalejas looked through the keyhole, whistling through his teeth. After a few minutes, the recruit came out and was questioned by the committee.

The room was so gloomy that at first I didn't notice there was anyone else in it. Then, as my eyes grew accustomed to the semi-darkness, I thought something moved in the corner. I realised that a back was facing me, as broad as a hippopotamus's back.

'Well, little soldier,' said a deep voice, 'what are you waiting for?'

I walked forward, still unable to see properly.

'Lord God almighty, they say there are no bad soldiers in Spain, but I can't promise you a place in heaven.'

She pushed the shutter open and a shaft of moonlight fell across the room between us. The face looking at me in the mirror was so fat I could hardly make out a feature. Her breathing sounded like a carpenter planing wood. The dress she wore was scarlet and flounced. As she rose and turned towards me, her arms flapped with hummocks of fat. Jewellery clinked. Everything swished against everything else as she moved over to the sink.

'Now let Pepita see you wash it,' she said.

She ran the tap.

'Come along, Pepita hasn't got all night.'

I stood in the patch of moonlight and stripped off my trousers.

'Mother and father of all the devils in hell!' she rumbled, 'but what are we supposed to do with *that*?'

She stood looking at me. 'I can't make a man of you with something like that,' she said. 'What is that Canalejas up to, sending me this kind of trash?'

She peered again.

'Almost like a . . . ' she looked up at me.

I smiled and nodded. Suddenly the broadest of smiles was creasing her features. She crossed herself.

'Holy Mother of God,' she said, thoughtfully. 'You're not a . . . girl, are you?'

I smiled, not knowing what to say, but feeling very relieved.

She held her index finger over her lips. It turned into a thumb that jerked towards the door.

'And Canalejas thinks you are a . . . ?'

I nodded.

A giggle welled up from somewhere in the acreage of fat. More tremors. Then Pepita was guffawing and holding her hand over her mouth.

She held her arms wide and I was folded against her rumbling chest. She stroked my hair.

'There there,' she said, 'you're safe with Pepita.'

We sat on the bed and in whispers I told her about Coimbras and the communion and that set her off again guffawing.

After she had subsided, she raised her index finger again. She motioned me to sit in the middle of the bed, then she placed her hands on my shoulders and pressed down. I had a sudden memory of Sergeant Diaz. Pepita was bouncing me on the bed. It creaked regularly. Then she threw back her head and mooed, exploding into high-pitched laughter.

The bed groaned once for every two creaks it gave out. 'Mother of God, Ramon,' she shouted, 'but that is heaven . . . oooh yes . . . yes Ramon more oh yes more please . . . '

Faster and faster she bounced me until there was a warning crack from the bed and Pepita began to wail no no no no nooo . . . bubbling at the end into a long low cry, and then silence.

Almost immediately, we did it again.

She flopped sweating on to the bed. The handle turned and when I looked up, the committee of four were standing at the foot of the bed.

'My God, Canalejas,' said Pepita, panting from her exertions and rolling her eyes at them, 'this one can teach you a trick or two.'

They looked at one another.

'Bring him again soon,' said Pepita, leering at me and lighting a cigarette, 'if that's how he entertains.'

All the way to the barracks, they asked me technical questions, which I answered as knowingly as I could. When we got back, Canalejas told the others that, no matter what he looked like, Puente was a man of *cojones*.

Pepita and I became friends. I often used to visit her on a Saturday night for a chat and a *copita*, her 'viva Jesus' as she called it. When I slipped out through the gate, the guard used to come to the door of the guardhouse.

'Ah, give her one for me!' he shouted.

When I left, Pepita insisted on giving me her medallion to the Virgin of Montserrat.

I walked the wrong way out of the Zoo-Bahnhof, opposite to the directions I'd been given. While I was wandering Kantstrasse, looking for someone to ask, Winfried drew up at the kerb and introduced himself. He was showing off, aiming his old red Opel like an arrow down Hohenzollerndamm.

'What's a pretty girl like you doing in Berlin?' he said at last in atrocious Spanish.

I fingered my passport. I wanted to bring it out and wave it at him. I wanted to yell, 'I'm a *man*, you stupid male bastard!'

But it was too late.

'How did you guess?' I asked, batting my eyelids.

'Oh I have spent a little while in Spain,' said Winfried modestly.

'I thought you must have done,' I said, simpering. 'Your Spanish is so good.'

We stopped at a bar for some drinks and started talking. Uncle Fausto had a cousin who worked in Siemens. He'd written to tell me that I might be able to get a job as a steel presser. After twenty-one months at Toledo, I didn't want to meet any more Spaniards, but I badly needed some money.

'As a secretary?' asked Winfried.

I nodded. 'I think a woman should work,' I said aggressively.

'Of course,' said Winfried.

After we'd had some beer and schnapps, we went back to his apartment in Schöneberg. He was impotent; but he was grateful to me, because I was sympathetic. We lay and smoked some cigarettes.

Winfried was a student of business methods at the Technical University. For two years he had been going each weekend to a *Mannesgruppe* to talk out his problem. He'd had relationships with three girls before, but I was the first one who had really made him trust her. He wanted me to stay with him.

I accepted his offer. That night he took me to a *Maibolle* party in

Charlottenburg. We'd only been there half an hour when Marianne Leiner slipped a hand down the back of my jeans. She asked me in faultless Spanish if I would dance with her. By the time Winfried came back with the refill of *Waldmeister*, I had her address and telephone number in my back pocket.

Marianne was frank with me, when I met her in Güntzelstrasse the following afternoon.

'*Chiquilla*,' she breathed, 'you're cute'.

She was the daughter of General Felix B. Leiner and had spent a long time in Mexico. She told me she could get me a job waitressing at the officers' club in Dahlem.

'Kind of a funny *shape*,' said Marianne when we were undressed, 'but real cute.'

In the evenings, I started going to German classes in Knesebeck-strasse. Wolfgang was our teacher. He took me down Bleibtreu-strasse and we had a beer at the '*Restez-fidele*'. Wolfgang is enormous, with great hands like bear's paws, and a shaggy head. On the way back to Schöneberg, he stopped the car just off Innsbruckerplatz and tried clumsily to kiss me.

Winfried was furious. He'd been waiting for several minutes back in Knesebeckstrasse. I explained I'd had a beer with my teacher. Winfried was jealous.

Wolfgang and I saw each other every evening in class. About a week later, I let him drive me over to his apartment in Kleistpark. He explained to me all the troubles he'd had with relationships. He was going to a *Mannesgruppe* to talk things out.

'Ramon,' he said, 'please I want you to stay with me tonight.'

My weeks were busy. Four nights a week I went to language classes. The rest were spent waitressing at the American officers' club and picking up tips. Two afternoons a week I spent with Marianne. One night a week I stayed over at Wolfgang's. This led to some painful scenes with Winfried. 'Just when I find a girl I like,' he said bitterly, 'she's unfaithful to me.'

One day I took the S-Bahn to work, but changing my mind, I stayed on and went over the border at the Friedrichstrasse checkpoint. I wandered along Unter den Linden, thinking about the complications of my life, and went into the restaurant. The waitress was looking at me. She smiled and I asked some questions about where she lived and what life was like in East Germany. When she brought me the bill, there was a note tucked inside it, asking me to wait for her at closing time.

I wandered back. Ursula was sitting alone on a restaurant chair in the middle of the avenue. She asked me if I'd like to come back to her house in the suburbs. We went to a small beer-house and then back to her apartment. She gave me coffee and *Apfeltorte* and sat by me on the sofa. I put my arm round her. After a while we stopped talking and started to kiss.

'You're shy,' she said.

'I have a problem,' I said, 'I'm thinking of going to a *Mannesgruppe* to sort it out.'

I heard a lot about Evelyn Lily Newcombe from the wives at the officers' club. Over their evening highballs at the Transport Section table, they recommended her to one another. Consultant gynaecologist at the American Military Hospital, and the author of *An Encyclopaedia of Infant Mortality*, 'Doctor Lily' was an authority.

Last week I managed to scrape enough money together for a consultation. I telephoned her and she invited me over to her house in Königen-Luise Strasse.

We talked. She examined me. Then went back to her roses. She snipped the stems one by one and placed them in the empty vase, while she thought about my question.

'If you mean,' she said at last, ' "Am I really male or female?" the answer is not so simple.'

A tiny hunchback as frail as a bird, Doctor Lily perched behind her walnut desk, her polished brogues dangling short of the floor. I looked up to the gigantic blow-up on the wall behind her of an infant's face, brimming with normality. There was something about it which reminded me of El Caudillo.

'I confess,' she said, 'I never thought I'd live to see an adult condition like yours. In fact, I didn't know for sure whether it was possible for a human organism to survive under such circum-stances. To live for a few minutes is rare. The incinerators of any large lying-in hospital will tell you that. There are usually severe accompanying adrenal deficiencies. To have reached the age of twenty-six is a miracle. To look as healthy and (may I say it?) as attractive as you do is . . . must be . . . an absolutely unique set of circumstances.'

'Please Dr Newcombe,' I said, 'just tell me what I really am. Am I male?'

She shook her head.

'Am I female?'

'No.'

'I'm a hermaphrodite then.'

'I'm afraid not,' said Dr Newcombe.

'What's left?' I asked. 'Am I nothing?'

'Strictly speaking, a hermaphrodite has both sets of organs simultaneous present. You have, as far as I can determine, one set. You're a pseudohermaphrodite. The real question, though, is still unanswered.'

'What's that?' I asked nervously.

'Which *kind* of pseudohermaphrodite are you? Let me explain.'

She motioned me up to the desk and opened a drawer.

'Now look at these.'

She took out two photographs and laid them down on the desk. She swivelled them round with the tips of her crinkled brown fingers.

'What sex do you think these are?' she asked.

I looked from one to the other. They were both close-ups of the pelvic area and genitalia. I looked from one to the other. They were identical.

'They're female,' I said.

She shook her head.

'Wrong. These are photographs of pseudohermaphrodite mal-formations of the genital area in different foetuses. The right hand one is female, and mortality occurred after several hours. The left hand one is male, and lived two days. They look identical, but they're completely different. Their malformations, if you like, imitate one another so perfectly that without autopsy it's impossible to tell them apart.'

'What's the difference,' I said. 'Why not call them normal and have done with it?'

Her adenoidal, baritone voice rasped with irritation. 'Hypertrophy of the clitoris,' she barked angrily, 'is not a matter of politics or philosophy. It's a physical condition, sometimes associated with the absence of the vagina or a concealed vaginal orifice, which leads to the erroneous assumption that the infant is a hypospadic male. On very rare occasions, as might be in your case, the urethra even penetrates the clitoris and produces a structure closely resembling a penis.'

'What's a hypospadic male?' I asked.

'Hypospadia is the commonest malformation of the male genital organs. It's the result of the incomplete or abnormal fusion of the urethral folds on the inferior surface of the genital tubercle. In its mild forms, the urethral orifice is located under the glans, near the attachment of the prepuce. But the condition can be more severe. In its complete form, the urethral orifice is located at the junction of the penis and the scrotum. With such a severe defect, the *corpora cavernosa* are frequently smaller than normal and the penis is reduced. Sometimes it is mistaken for a hypertrophied clitoris, especially if the testes are undescended, the median raphe of the scrotum is indented, and the scrotum itself – as in the case of this left hand photograph – is bilobate.'

'Are you saying . . . '

'I'm saying that on the preliminary examination I've conducted, it's almost certain that you're a pseudohermaphrodite of the one kind or the other. But that it's impossible to ascertain your sex from external examination alone.'

'But what does that *mean*?'

'These are the facts. When we've done some X-rays and glandular tests, we'll be in a position to perform the appropriate operation. Meanwhile I advise you to take a holiday in the country and forget about it. Once we've determined your sex, we can regularise you.'

She slipped down off her chair and reached up on to the desk, sweeping the rose clippings to the edge with the palm of her hand.

'It's nothing,' she said. 'The operation's quite a simple one . . . in either case.'

CRUSOE

Let him who can arise, withdraw into himself, forgo all that is known by the eyes, turn aside for ever from the bodily beauty that was once his joy. He must not hanker after the graceful shapes that appear in bodies, but know them for copies, for traceries, for shadows, and hasten away towards that which they bespeak. For if one pursue what is like a beautiful shape moving over water – Is there not a myth about just such a dupe, how he sank into the depths of the current and was swept to nothingness?

(Plotinus, *Enneads*)

1. BLEIBTREU CAFÉ

That's what I do, walk back up the beach into the trees, nothing on my mind except my curriculum. This morning, I have to go to Belfort to see my scarecrows. Up through the steps I cut in the rock, up through the path in the top thicket. They're still there, of course. As if they wouldn't be. But sometimes I wake in the middle of the night with a start, thinking they're walking off. Or in the day, while sewing a new pair of trousers, I look up as the thought strikes me: supposing they've got down from their pyramids of birch-bark and twigs and, together with their new friends, the birds, are feasting on my crops? Then I can smile and go back to my sewing. With their hooked beaks, wings spread in an attitude of instant take-off, and three foot, ochre-stained pupils raking the heavens, what crow, passing never so high, in the fullness of his insolence, would dare let fall one niggardly quark of lime? I smile and go back to my sewing.

But there are other things which do upset me. Sometimes my thoughts are not so easy to soothe. I have the feeling, as acute as if a fly were inching about on my extremities, that someone is setting foot on my land. Unknown hands are breaking my hurdles. I can't rest then until I have done my rounds. I return, exhausted, caked with mud and half-asleep, dimly aware that I have not been honest with myself. There's a corner I've neglected. It's a corner that originally took me months to fence off. I flop down on the rush matting. But I can't sleep. My ears are assailed by the cries, tormenting in their urgency, of my nannies, whose udders are bursting because I've neglected them to go on my rounds.

But these thoughts are only a mundane version of others beyond them, almost unthinkable in their refinement. I dream of a system of alarm bells attached to every leaf in every tree, each one directly connected to my cerebral cortex. I'm afraid Birnam Wood will come to Dunsinane without my knowing.

Feelings like this are accompanied by irrepressible urges to reconnoitre. I run, leaping from tummock to tummock, boulder to boulder, as sure-footed as one of my goats, to the top of the cliff above Belfort. I must *be* a goat – for which, these days, I could easily pass – and be unaware of the echo of my steps crackling through the pines, unaware, as I turn the corner along the cliff walk, of the tense, panting shadow that speeds in front. When I get to the spot, I don't do what I supposedly meant to do: look through the telescope. I circle aimlessly about, having scanned the whole crescent of the bay out of the corner of my eye, plucking the leaves and branches with the idleness of a boy in spring coming home from school.

I wince as I perform this deception: it's hard to be casual here, when you're casual all the time. You've bought up your stocks of real casualness. So you have to go on to pretending to be casual. It's all a matter of confidence.

I camouflaged the telescope in a bush, so effectively that, at times like this, I myself forget where it is. In all these 'aimless' pluckings and whistlings and cries, I'm keeping my eye open for the peep of its eye-piece. When I find it, I don't edge nearer like an inexperienced thief. I don't go near it at all. I've placed a dummy telescope there too, in another almost identical bush.

It is constructed from pieces of bamboo, sheathed (telescopically) one inside the other. Through its imitation lenses – the stretched membranes from a pig's kidneys glued over the end of each section – one can see absolutely nothing. That is an exaggeration. To be precise, a powerfully restricted version of what one sees with the naked eye. After an hour or two of sitting pretending to have a picnic until my stomach is groaning from the mangoes I haven't eaten, or lying chewing at a straw and staring at the heavens until my neck is stiff from the effort of idleness, I make a dash for the dummy and 'look' through it, squinting one eye for verisimilitude. The other is anointed by a soothing blur. Then, aglow with the awareness of the real telescope snug in its bush, I can descend by the back path. Always, after the success of this operation, by the back path.

But sometimes it's not successful. Sometimes, after hours of tooling round waiting for the right moment, I make my final dash and squint, only to recoil in confusion. The waves lap my retina. I have looked through the Zeiss by mistake. Once, to my horror, I saw a sail moving behind the reef. Torn between the desires to focus and obliterate, I wrenched at the eyepiece. It resolved itself into the circlings of a condor. When there is an error in my preparations, then danger occurs.

That's when I descend, panic in my heart, by the front path, noticing nothing as I worm over the rope bridge, my glance deviating neither right nor left until the white pales of my pallisade come into view. I open it by the gate I made, which I close and carefully lock behind me with the lock I made from scraps of suitcases. I'm in the outer pound. Now I must take care to avoid the traps I've set, their bamboo stakes set at the requisite slant, which lurk under the innocuous carpet of palm-leaves. The plan I carry with me in a special pouch in my trousers, together with my box containing its single match. But I can't use it. In times of panic, my fingers are all thumbs and the pouch is inaccessible to them. Using the knowledge that my traps are there as an incentive to memory, I thread my way between them. When it is not panic stations, then I use the back path.

There is one exception to this. Harvest time, when I have to bring in my little store of maize. Then I take out my plan and consult it, because I need more room to cross when I'm dragging my cart behind me. This yearly consultation serves to refresh my memory for the coming year.

When I've crossed my outer pound, I come to my outworks, once the contents of my pits, now made into a system of ramparts and coped by a foot-high tangle of poisonous thorns. There is an opening, so inconspicuous that sometimes, even with the plan fluttering in my hand, I have difficulty finding it. Then I'm in my yard. I've cobbled the floor with stones from the beach, and the whole in every detail resembles an English farmyard, even down to the balsa-wood model of a Light Sussex cockerel, caught in the act of flying at me each time I enter.

I've never had cause to regret my thoroughness, but on one occasion I came near to it. It happened that panic stations and harvest time came simultaneously. When I reached the pallisade, the gate seemed so cunningly dovetailed into the woodwork that I almost imagined someone else had constructed it. I ran up and down from one identical section of the fence to another, wringing my hands, my mind a blank. In the end, I wheeled the cart round in front of me and drove it full tilt at my fence, like a battering ram. Before I had time to think, we had flattened the pallisade, skated, miraculously unscathed, across the outer pound, and burst through the ramparts into the stackyard, burying the Light Sussex under a mound of earth. From beneath the cart, I looked back at the trail of destruction I had just wrought, and felt it like the shock of a fresh cut.

Even now, in times of ordinary panic, as I approach my pallisade I can feel the twinge of the memory like an old scar. But normally my entries are not of this nature. Normally I descend by the back path sweetly into my hutch proper. The penetralium, sewn together out of two parachutes, is a cool, light area, reminiscent of a marquee at an English country fête. It bivouacs the original cave entrance. Inside, it is colder and mustier. At the back of this room is a rope-ladder, by means of which one enters the true recess. I ascend, and pull up, after me, the ladder. I drop it on the other side of the wall and climb down. Then I unhook it and stow it in a hole in the rock, taking care to cover the hole with a stone.

For some time the conspicuousness of this stone troubled me, because, through its prominent position and exotic nature, it seemed to announce that it was a piece of camouflage. I placed a false stone a few yards away, not a stone at all in fact, but a root vegetable, hacked up to look like a stone. After a time, as vegetables do, it went rotten and ceased to perform its role as decoy-stone. Instead it went green and smelt rank, thereby calling attention to itself. I replaced it with another. This also became obvious after a while. For some time I was at a loss until the expediency occurred to me of concealing the ladder sometimes behind the decoy-stone, and sometimes behind the real stone. At this scheme, I grew intellectually proud and longed to conceal it in other places. Why bother with these stupid stones? Why not just hide it anywhere I felt like? This I did.

The rest of the day I spent digging freely in my back room, gloating over the simplicity, the elegance of this idea which had removed, at a single stroke, a burden from my shoulders. In the evening, I grew hungry and arrived back at the foot of the wall, only to discover that I had forgotten where I had hidden it with such *élan*. For what could have been several days, I sat there, quivering with cold, starving, and racking my brains. I grew so dizzy and weak that, for long periods of time, I forgot what it was I was supposed to be remembering.

For a time, my memory fed me on *fettucine alla marinara*, *rognons de veau aux tomates*, *Gemüse Suppe*, Hungarian goulash, and roast lamb stuffed with sprigs of rosemary and thyme, and garnished with freshly ground, horseradish sauce. At first there was a period in which I ate, separately, slowly, and with contentment, all these things, discriminately chewing each mouthful. But my appetite drove my memory like a charioteer, until the beginning of the next dish began to coagulate into the end of the last.

Soon I was in the grip of hyperbole. One meal – albeit five courses, and consumed over a period of five hours – could do nothing for me. I began to eat all the meals I could remember together, stuffing into my mouth, simultaneously, great pieces of herring, their tails hanging out over my lips, laced with cubed mango and curry sauce, or forkfuls of pig's tripe from Yorkshire, creamed with the oysters I had in Bebinje. I stuffed myself with a potpourri of condensed occasions, wolfing down in the composite restaurant of my mind meals which in actuality had been consumed over three-quarters of the living globe, sometimes a quarter of a century apart. I tried to substitute intensity for duration, but this was a step which, once taken, could not be gone back on.

By now, my appetite had grown so distended that I began to come to the end of my memories of meals. When I tried to repeat my old stand-bys, I found that my memory had begun to take them for granted, or for eaten, and they were over before they were begun on. At last, under severe pressure from my appetite, my memory began to reject them and, in the equivalent of a kind of mental vomiting, one by one, and then several together, they went out of existence, as if borne off into the darkness by a series of invisible, but malicious waiters, white steaming disks shrinking into spots and popping out, leaving the illusion of an aftertaste on my swollen tongue, which was bristling like a sow's back with frustration. Recall proved impossible.

My appetite died at that point, leaving me only its memory. Salivating freely, I entered various restaurants in the capital cities of the world. But each time I set foot in the palm-strewn lobby, pushed tentatively at the revolving door, or even stood outside on the pavement reading the menu, the premises briskly emptied of all the apparatus of a restaurant; the cries of the cooks and the clangs of the kitchen growing faint and silent; the spattling rings turning cold; the candles guttering; the customers wiping themselves out like slogans off a window, shrinking into collections of lines and squiggles and then, with the echo of a belch, disappearing altogether, leaving me standing in the middle of an empty building.

Sometimes they didn't altogether disappear, but employed ruses to avoid my custom. One in particular – the Bleibtreu café – had the effrontery to turn into a furniture shop. As I approached, whole companies of people, in reality customers in what five microseconds earlier had been a crowded restaurant, were lying on beds, pretending to be testing the springs, or lounging in armchairs in hastily adopted postures of extreme casualness, the waiters still with the candle grease on their trousers, posing, without a shred of credibility, as sales assistants.

I called to them, it's OK, game's up now. Just bring me some minestrone to start with, and a pork chop. Oh and I'll have a bottle of beer with it . . . Oh, and can you bring the minestrone right away because I'm rather . . . Silence. Stony faces, not a smile anywhere. The customers, still in their groups of four and six, went on bouncing the beds and smiling at one another. The assistants moved to and fro across the carpeted floor, murmuring as they went. In desperation I went up to one of them and tore at his garments. Come off it, my friend, I shouted, you are a waiter, I know you are . . . Look at this candle grease on your trousers . . . And . . . I plunged my hand into his trousers pocket . . . I can prove it, I yelled, as my fingers closed round his little pencil and pad. But I was suddenly in the midst of a crowd of people who wrenched the pad out of my hand, leaving a tiny corner of it between my fingers, and lifted me high above their heads. I could have been taken for a triumphant sports star, for the moment before they hurled me out on to the pavement.

The glass doors slid to and they resumed their charade. I went back, again and again, and hammered on the windows. They called the police. I devoted all my efforts to trying to catch them out. They were so quick to change, that I could never quite see it happen. I sneaked up through the arcade opposite. I peered through the window of the souvenir shop. I even sidled into the butcher's further down the street and hovered in the doorway, pretending to examine the pork chops in the window. I didn't even notice what they were, so single-minded was my purpose. Because if I'd thought about it, I could have bought a pork chop there and then, and saved myself a lot of trouble. Why bother with all this stupid restaurant business anyway?

Because there comes a point where justice has to be upheld, I told myself. I was not a primitive animal, a slave to my appetite. I wanted to prove it to myself. I wanted to catch them at it. It was obvious that the souvenir shop woman and the butcher were on the look out for me. They were equipped with walkie-talkies under their aprons and smocks.

I tried getting a taxi and driving to the restaurant. The taxi driver looked at me askance. For a moment I thought he was going to say something, then he shrugged and clocked up his meter. Later I heard him talking to them over the radio. I was not surprised when we drew up outside and the change had been fully completed. I tried riding by on a bus. But the bus driver saw me getting on and flashed his lights to the driver of the bus in front. Even as we fled by, I saw they had managed to change.

Then a court order arrived through the post. They had succeeded in obtaining an injunction, restraining me from molesting them. Rolling up my sleeves, I decided to become litigious. If they wanted to play at that game, they would get their comeuppance.

I took my scrap of waiter's pad to a lawyer. The Trades Descriptions Act. The Fire Regulations. There must be something we could get them with. Right on, said my smart-alec lawyer. They lured you into the restaurant with false advertising, and then tried to sell you a bed . . . After three years of legal battles, the judge of the Supreme Court ordered that they should permanently become a restaurant again, and that they should pay the cost of the case. Moreover, he stipulated that they should serve me with minestrone, beer, and a pork chop and – wise old man in his wig and robes, he threw me a wink in court – a vegetable salad, followed by pistachio ice-cream, followed by a Camembert so ripe it was crawling out of its box and oozing all over the table-cloth.

To a fanfare of interior trumpets, heedless of the midday traffic, I marched down the main street and sailed up to the front door, preparing to sit down at what was to be my usual table by the window. But the windows were chalked over with crosses, and everywhere there were TO LET notices pasted. One letter, cobwebbed and askew, remained from the name of the furniture store. Outraged, I rushed into the hairdressers next door, where I recognised several of the waiters, now working as assistant hairdressers. The restaurant, forced by my investigations to pretend continuously that it was a furniture store, had gone bankrupt . . .

At this point I remembered my stone pantry, on the same side of the wall as myself. There I had a store of peanuts, laid up in case of seige. The tunnel which leads to it is long and narrow and dark. It is not very inviting. Perhaps this is why I forgot it. But perhaps this is also why I remembered it, because whatever I think is most uninviting to others, is most valuable to me.

2 FOOTPRINT

Belfort is only my pseudo-hutch.

I don't live there any more.

Its details have become, instead of the loving stamp collection they started out by being, an incrustation of worthless picturesque. I feel each one personally. A good-job-well-done turned heavy and sour. Turned give-away. All was well. I hammered and sang. In the evenings I sat, my hand resting on the real porch, listening to the cicadas. Then one morning I was wandering along the beach looking for crabs, when I came across a human footprint in the sand. At first, I thought it was a rockpool and ignored it. But then I saw what it was, a large solitary footprint.

I looked up and down. I circled it, my heart beating. Were there others? I couldn't find any. I sat down and regarded it. Did it perhaps date from before I arrived here? Not very likely. It looked fresh enough. Why hadn't it washed away with the rains and the wind and the tide and the shifting of the infinite grains of sand and the mating rituals of the crabs and the burrowings of the little mites? Because the closer I looked at it, the older it looked. Now it looked both fresh *and* old.

Certain portions of the earth's crust erode and other portions remain. Perhaps it wasn't a footprint at all, but a piece of erosion. A minuscule version of the Grand Canyon. It just happened, by one of those coincidences of which nature is such a brimming repository, to look like a human foot. In fact, it was a configuration of the elements. The meeting point for hundreds of years of wind and sand . . .

But as my awe rose and I gazed at it more intently, I saw in it, quite distinctly, the imprint of a corn. Could nature produce corns as well? Could the elements, after hundreds of years of random blowing and raining and hailing, actually have succeeded in putting the corn on the foot? I imagined all the times the corn had been imprinted in some insignificant patch of scrub, underneath a liana, missing the foot by a mile.

If this were true of a corn, what of all the other things that could have happened? It had the right number of toes on it. It was a coherent right foot. Gingerly, I put my own in it. It fitted perfectly. But was this hypothesis likely, in this place where the temperature hardly ever varied, and no erosion, of anything to speak of, took place? It would have been different if I'd found it in my cave.

The thought sent me scurrying back to Belfort to see if there were any footprints there. I combed the island. I scoured the tracks of goats and wild pigs. But all I could find was this one solitary piece of evidence of a human foot. Why had the marauder not come further than the beach? I took to watching, waiting for him to return. I watched for days, never taking my eyes from the spot where the footprint lay, except to scan the horizon.

At last, my vigilance was rewarded. At first it was a speck. Then the boat grew larger, cutting smartly across the bay. It was an outrigger. On deck were three men, all a dusky-brown colour, clad in loin cloths. As they entered the lagoon, they began to paddle in the frantic unison only achieved by people in tapestries and friezes before the advent of perspective. Their speed was immense, the prow raised out of the water by their impetus.

As the boat swung round and grounded in the shallows, a quarrel broke out among its occupants. One didn't want to get out. In the end, the other two pushed him. They pointed to the spot, determined by a complex alignment of sun and palms. One of them thrust a brush into his hand. He hopped across to the spot and stood, an expression of great discomfort on his face, like a stork, until his brown foot had almost disappeared from view. Then he hopped back. After each step, turning and brushing the sand. One of them leaned out with another brush and, as he climbed back on board, carefully brushed away his last step. Then he pushed off the boat with the brush handle. I ran down to the beach.

Of course. Wherever there was a footprint, there should be a number of small holes. There weren't any. But whatever they pushed off with should have left a mark. Perhaps the sand was weak there, just at the point where the brush handle had gone in. Maybe they had a one-legged man, whom they brought, whenever it rained, to renew his footprint. Or a two-legged man who lived throughout the dry season near the beach. As soon as it rained, he got on to a kind of ski-lift and swung down over the beach from one end to the other, dipping a solitary right foot into the sand at the lowest point of his trajectory and swinging up again and landing on the other side of the beach. Or an enormous one-legged woman, an Amazonian type of person, making her forays, her foot sinking deep into the sand and rock beneath her weight.

Something was in error. But I couldn't trace the error back to its origin. Fifty years ago it might have happened like that, but not now.

Two boats came across the bay. One the painted outrigger and the other a motor boat, in the prow of which stood a man with a loud-hailer. The man shouted to the occupants of the outrigger in a language I couldn't understand. They took out of a locker a plaster cast of a foot on a long pole. When the outrigger grounded as before, the man gave instructions from the motor boat through the loud-hailer. The men on the outrigger pushed the cast of the naked foot into the preordained spot in the sand.

Their victim had died and in the meantime they had taken a death-mask of his foot. But why did they need to have the same foot? Especially if the footprint needed renewing? They could have any foot they chose. They could renew it with the smallest and daintiest foot of their tribe. A baby's footprint. But a baby's footprint could be confused with an animal's. In order to be at all effective, it would have to be a larger foot. Perhaps they were a tribe with particularly small feet, living as they did most of the time on boats and not needing to walk about very much. They would naturally preserve the largest foot they could find, even if it did happen to belong to a one-legged man.

But it was not just a piece of utility after all. Perhaps he was sacred, the one-legged man. They must create exactly the same footprint, even long after its owner had passed away, in order that rain should occur, or their women should keep on bearing children. But it was not just symbolic either. Or there was no way of distinguishing.

Perhaps they did it for a number of times, a prelude inscrutably repeated to a formula and then, at high tide, or when the moon was in its seventh house, they were going to come in enormous numbers, twenty or thirty of their ships, running up the beach, obliterating the footprint with their tracks. Without exploring the island in the least they were going to seize me at the entrance to my hutch. This was a diversionary ruse to allow some of them, while I was occupied with the business of the footprint, to land on the other side of the island, leaving no footprints at all, and come straight into my hutch. And survey it.

I went straight back to Belfort, sick at heart, leaving the footprint where it was, the waves washing gently over it. I walked to and fro in my parlour. What had happened to my garden was comparable to the advent of the serpent. All my fortifications were a useless parody. Supposing they had landed already, using the footprint trick. Then they had seen my goats, my crops, my scarecrows, my flag flying at half-mast for the death of my parrot. There was little point in destroying Belfort. That would be more obvious than retaining it. I looked round. I felt soiled. All my labour, gone to waste. But what was labour? No one would pay me for it.

I looked at my kitchen. Let it stand. It could be my *Marie Celeste*. I would put some food out before I left. I went out on to the porch and ran my hand along the rail. It shrank into the two-dimensional: the whole of my little civilisation, fences, ditches, traps, recesses, was suddenly no more real than the set for a cowboy picture. Let it stand.

That's how I came to climb the slopes of this extinct volcano and raise my cabin here. It looks small, but I've learnt my lesson. It's not as small as it seems, because I have hollowed out a space in the rock under the floorboards of the kitchen, and this is where I really live.

3   TREAT THY NEIGHBOUR AS THYSELF

When I woke, it was evening and the flies were rejoicing inside the fuselage. Perhaps he was alive.

Hodges, it had to be Hodges.

As I scrambled into the wreckage, I was amazed to see him move. Another person. Alive. He was struggling to get to his feet. The thoughts raced like meteors through my mind. We could be neighbours. I never liked him. It would be hell. But we could have separate huts, build stout walls in between us, reach agreements. Share out the land. I would have more, of course, because I was out first.

He turned. Under his torn overalls the muscles seemed to be rippling. I had the sensation of power. His elbows appeared to be moving up and down his arms, as if they had become retractable. The same with his knees. In his chest, I could see the bulge of his heartbeat, actually pounding. I greeted him, Frank are you all right?

His eyes opened brightly and he winked broadly at me. I shouted with laughter. Had I had a cap, I would have thrown it in the air. But then, as he began to come towards me, he did something that wiped the smile from my face. He put out a long, smooth, dark-pink tongue. What was he doing with his tongue out? I stepped back as he came nearer. Why were his movements so peculiar? I retreated.

In a flash, the whole picture dissolved. Hodges' eyes were open indeed, but above each one of them, squatting in his hair, was a rat, and these rats had Hodges' eyelashes in their little teeth and were holding them open. Instead of a tongue, a long smooth tail hung down from between his lips. Hodges gave out sounds, but they were the sounds of this rat, greedily excavating his vocal chords. His arms and legs flailed wildly at the activity beneath his clothing.

I ran back as Hodges began to move across the floor not crawling, not walking, not rolling, not seeing, not grinning, not holding out his hand to be shaken, as he *appeared* to be. Yet he did all these things, his clothing undulating, popping, bulging with the frenzy underneath it. With a whole series of sighs and crackings and groans and rustles he went close by me, half on the floor, half upright, limbs shooting everywhere. Sometimes he seemed to be on his side on the ground, sometimes on tiptoe, head flung back, arms flying, in a gesture of rubbery supplication. Then he went into a forward roll, head tucked, buttocks tipping high into the air, and stopped. I could see the scurrying plainly under his overalls at the back and bottom. It increased in intensity until finally he rolled over forwards and began his progress again. The last I saw of him was his back bobbing in the bushes at the edge of the clearing as he vanished.

For a long time the incident died completely. Resolutely, I forgot every part of it. I plunged into project after project. But as I dug and wove and built, I began to require certain pieces of equipment. Whenever I required them, I knew where they were to be found. I started going back to the site. I saw nothing. I was encouraged. I took everything, even the outside metal for my heat exchanger and my Trombe Wall. Still I hadn't let in the memory again of what happened.

At first, I stole like a fugitive to the Piper, looking furtively round and scuttled away with what I required under my arm. But I soon grew bolder, openly dismantling the engine and ripping out the polythene and perspex in my excitement.

One bright morning I was walking through my wood, on my way to dump a bucketful of slurry. I was singing and swinging the bucket, thinking of nothing but a photograph of myself singing and swinging the bucket, when his body rolled out of the trees and lay all over the path. I shouted aloud. In my confusion I emptied the stinking mess from the bucket all over myself, and ran blindly into the wood. I ran for several miles, moans escaping from my lips. What it was I couldn't think. What had happened I couldn't assess. It had no meaning. I ran to my hutch, pulled up my rope ladder, and crouched deep within in the cold and dark. But it was clear, luminous, every frame arrested in slow motion, every movement separated from every other, repeating itself over and over again. I tried to think, but my thinking tables wouldn't come.

Pro	Contra
!	?
?	!!!!

Did this thing really happen? It was unlikely. Several years had elapsed, according to my calculations, since the incident of Hodges. It must be some form of delusion. But it was useless to behave as if it hadn't happened, because my memory kept flooding with images. I might as well be practical. To all intents and purposes, it had happened. I had also to assume that it was out there, waiting to happen again. Or happening again somewhere, even now, without me. Not needing me at all, to go through the brightly-lit motions of its happening. I was a mere accident. I had just come upon it.

But then the question was, where would it happen again? What was I going to do? I clutched my skins to me and cried aloud at the thought, Could it come in here, into my hutch, and *happen*? I clenched my memory like a fist, but the bright pictures ran out between my fingers. I erected a door in my mind – substantial, bristling with bolts – and pushed it to with its first click. But it was too late. I'd already noticed that the door down the corridor was ajar. I went to close that one, but as I reached it, I saw through the crack, the flash of an overall disappearing round the next one. I sprinted to that and pulled it open. The corridor was empty, the door at the end was swinging, off the latch. This was no good. It was silly. It could go on for ever. I shut it resolutely and turned round to walk back. The door I had last shut behind me swung open. Through it, I saw the next door opening on to the diminished but brightening square of the next, which contained within it its own embryo-square, and in the centre of that, a tiny, flailing silhouette.

I spent all day trying to coax it nearer. Making a dash sometimes towards it. Every time, we just covered another corridor each. What could I do? I had to watch. I couldn't walk the other way, knowing what I did. It wouldn't be practical. It was practical to be *there*.

I shivered. Where could I find food in these corridors? Perhaps I was going to die in there, between these metallic-grey walls with the paint peeling off them. The tiny animated silhouette growing fainter, as I sank to the ground, still gazing at it. Minutes passed. I whimpered. Minutes again. Tiny flickerings, almost out of sight. No change. I was getting very weak. How long this went on for I have no idea. But as I gazed, a rush of anger overtook me. I felt my eyes like pebbles in the front of my head, my veins stood out as I opened my mouth wide and roared at the top of my voice

H . . . O . . . D . . . G . . . E . . . S . . .

Instantly I felt the morning sun on my face, the bucket of slurry in my hand, and smelt the wood and turned the corner and sure enough he rolled out and lolled everywhere. He smelt terrible. Half his face seemed to have gone.

I adopted the casual approach. Oh Hello Frank, I said, passing by on the other side. I walked on swinging the bucket and a few yards later he rolled out again in front of me. I skirted him, accordingly, whistling. He repeated it. I laughed. Couldn't he think of anything else? Each time he did it, it became sillier. Huh, I said, is that all you can manage, Frank?

It was all starting to get on my nerves. Ignoring him didn't really work either. It was all just a form of attention-getting. Even if I ignored him, he knew I was paying him enough attention to ignore him. I was supporting him. I decided to change tack.

The next time he did it, I hurled the bucket of slurry over him. He pretended to take no notice. I grabbed him by the scruff of the neck. Unfortunately, I grabbed a rat's back instead of his neck. But I threw the fat rat as far as I could into the trees. Come off it, Frank, I said between my teeth, looking squarely into his half a face, I know you've got arms down inside those fucking overalls, what is it you want?

He was in such a bad condition that speech was well beyond him. What could I do? I couldn't leave him, because he wouldn't leave me. The only alternative was to take him home with me. At least I knew where he was then.

For some time I had the unpleasant experience of living with him. I had never liked him when he was alive. Death had not improved him. Unreality had made him even worse. Ostentatiously, I paid attention to him. Every day he got stronger and more trivially objectionable. I nursed him in this way, untiringly, hoping for some kind of harmony. A vain hope. Frank got very well. After his throat had healed up, we even managed one or two hoarse passages of dialogue. But one evening I came in from the fields and my hutch was full of a peculiar smell that I recognised instantly. It was the odour of Frank, going off. It was the stink of Frank, sulking. At first I didn't understand. I sat down in my rocking chair and looked at him in disgust.

What's the matter, Frank? After all my nursing, feeding, tucking him up at night? How could he? It just didn't make sense. But then, as he went before my eyes from bad to worse, and from worse to excruciating, I began to see the point. Frank liked my hutch. He liked it very much. He liked the land around it. This was Frank's way of telling me he wanted a home of his own. I objected to his methods and I told him so. But I saw immediately the advantages of setting Frank up with his own place, if possible, right on the other side of the island.

So I gave him a piece of land. He was sweetness and light. Every morning for several months, we set out and worked together on his site. I lit a huge bonfire on top of the cliff and got the rocks very hot. Then, using the water we had carried up from the sea, doused it abruptly. The sudden drop in temperature fissured the rock. We hacked out the split pieces and repeated the operation until we'd reached a good way into the cliff and could make a cave there. It was the perfect fortress. I began to feel envious.

Frank was delighted. While we worked, we had long conversations about all the people Frank didn't like. I gave him goats to start his own herd. We arranged to co-operate with signal fires in the event of invasion.

All went well for about a year. We sometimes met along the fence and talked. But then came a period when I didn't see Frank at all. I didn't bump into him anywhere. I began to wonder what was the matter. I set out to find out, but long before I reached his hutch, I knew. I could smell him. When I climbed the steps and got inside he was about ten per cent gone.

All right, what did he want? But I answered my own question, before Frank could brush the maggots from his lips. Frank was starting to get greedy. Frank wanted more land, didn't he? I realised what the game was now. Frank was out to get everything. For a moment, I was tempted to go along with him and let him take me over, lock, stock and barrel. Then I could use him as the decoy if we were invaded. He couldn't have Belfort, because he knew about that already. But he could have this cabin. Or just stay in his own. He'd be difficult for them to pin down. He was the perfect guerilla. He could keep them going for years, appearing where they most expected him. But this was not the time for jokes. Something had to be done.

I meditated as I went on my rounds, trying not to sniff the breeze. The situation was limitless. What would he do when he'd got all my property? Something even more unpleasant. He could switch on and start going bad at any moment. I'd never have any peace again. There'd be no end to the concessions he'd wring from me. I knew it was myself that was keeping him in such good shape. That was the irony of the situation. But what could I do? I couldn't let him go. I couldn't ignore him. That was what my policy of appeasement was all about. I was committed to that now.

Maybe I should have taken a hard line and gone on ignoring him in the first place. But I was too rational for that kind of behaviour. But *was* I committed? Was I really unable to go back on it all? Each moment, the idea grew stronger. The only way I was ever going to stop this was to deal with Frank, finally. It was going to be hard. To detach a parasite is the first step, but it's also the hardest. It had to be done. But where would I find the concentration to go through with the rest of it? A rehearsal would ruin the scheme. The surprise element was essential. If he got an inkling, he'd cling on stronger and stronger, and each step I took against him would confirm his existence.

I went back to my hutch. I took pencil in hand and, on the top of the last sheet of the Piper's log book, wrote:

Ask the neighbour in

I broke down. I couldn't do it. Quick, or he knew and it was all over. I crossed it out, my hand sweating on to the paper like a nervous examination candidate's, and began again this time without stopping:

Lure the neighbour in on the pretext of a discussion about fencing, then shoot him in the brain with a .303. Some people use a captive bolt pistol, but I don't recommend this. He may, if he sees it, move away. A captive bolt has to be held close to the head and if he sees you holding one of these against his temple, he might turn his head to ask you what you're up to. With a .303 you can stand well back and shoot him through the hole you've made in the wall without him even noticing, which is the whole idea really. The traditional way is to stick him of course. But I would never ever do this, unless I had stunned him with a bullet first, or, failing that, a good swipe on the back of the neck with an axe. Although I see nothing wrong in killing them for meat, I see everything wrong in making neighbours suffer in this way. As soon as he's dropped, out from your cubby-hole and stick him. Squat down in front and stick the knife in just above the collar bone in the side of the neck. Push in a couple of inches and pull round to the back of the neck. This should sever the artery. Now watch out: a nervous reaction takes place. The neighbour appears to come to life and threshes about, so take care not to be scratched by his nails, as beginners often do. If you want the blood, you've got to be quick, some people slap a strap on his legs and haul him up on block and tackle before sticking. This enables you to catch the blood more easily and makes the neighbour drain better. Personally I don't like black pudding anyway. Now you've got to scrape your neighbour: a pretty ticklish business. The best method is to lay him on his side and pour boiling water over a small part of him. Keep pouring gently and from time to time try a hair or two with thumb and forefinger. When it starts to lift, scrape. Scrape like hell. Knives are all right, but better to use a sharpened saucepan-lid or a lawn-mower blade. Off comes his hair, off comes his skin, and no matter what colour your neighbour started off, he'll be as red as a beetroot when you've finished. The head is difficult; if necessary, set fire to some straw with methylated spirits, hold it over the flame to singe, and scrub with a wire brush. Then hang your neighbour. Behind the ankle is the Achilles' tendon. Cut a vertical slit down either side and prise it out with your fingers. Don't cut the leg above the hamstring as beginners do — this is barbarous and spoils the meat. Now, don't haul that neighbour off the ground till you've sawn through the sternum. Cut down to the breastbone with a clean knife and split it with a saw. If you try to do this after you've hung the man, all the guts will come flopping out and make the operation difficult. Then lay on to the fall of that tackle and heave away! Up goes your neighbour. Cut off his head (at the Atlas) and put it straight into brine. Before you've hauled him too high, cut round the bung. Cut round it so as to sever it from the neighbour, but don't whatever you do pierce the rectum. Tie a string round it to prevent the shit coming out. Now haul him up further to a convenient height and score a lightish cut from under the legs to your stick-cut in the neck. Don't cut through the abdominal wall! Cut right down, keeping the guts back from the knife with your hand. You don't want to pierce either them or the stomach. Now gently haul out rectum, penis, scrotum and all the guts, and flop the lot into a handy bowl. Rectum can be thrown to the dogs, but all the rest is edible useful stuff. Don't waste the guts. They need a wash, after which you should turn the intestines inside out. You can do this by inverting them on a smooth piece of bamboo. Scrape their mucus lining off with a knife on a board and get them quite clean and transparent. They'll come in for sausage casings. The bladder can be filled through a funnel with melted fat. It will harden and keep for months that way. The stomach makes excellent chitterlings. Turn it inside out, wash it, and lay it in dry salt until you want it. Don't waste the head or feet because they make delicious brawn. Rescue the liver, which you eat the same night. The heart (good for stuffing) should come away with the pluck. Hang it on a hook. The lungs are an extra treat for the dogs. Throw several buckets of water inside and outside the carcass, prop the belly open with a stick pointed at both ends, eat some fried liver, finish the home brew, off to bed.

The stillness after I laid down my pen has lasted to this minute. It is not absolute. Something moves in it. But to speak of Frank is not to resurrect him. Not as he was, anyway. The ruins of his hutch still stand on top of the cliff. To visit used to be a challenge: to invest these implements from a bygone age hanging on the walls, these armchairs made from crates, with any life at all. I climb the cliff steps, I hear the creak of the door, without emotion. I sniff deeply. Nothing but good sea air. I come back, not sobered by the effort of using my imagination historically, but elated by the irretrievability of the past.

4   POWER FROM THE BOTTOM

From my seat I can see across the clearing. I like to keep the door open these days. At night I like to look at the stars. They chasten me, these flaming balls of gas, but they comfort me too. If I want the door shut, I use a goat's-fat candle, or a reed taper. But I prefer the stars.

By day I can see my windmill, turning above the trees. It's not connected to anything now, but it still goes. I was proud of my 750 watts. Now I'm indifferent. I took the propeller from the Piper, but it didn't work unless the wind was low. I adapted it: centrifugal force works on the balance weights to overcome a set of springs attached to the hub shaft, so the blades feather automatically if the rotor overspeeds. A rubber belt made from fuselage-lining, set with aluminium teeth I made from tubular seat-legs, drives the aeroplane's alternator. Power is transmitted down the inside of the tower, through a conducting slip-ring and brush. Power, I don't use any more.

Originally, after I discovered that the Piper's batteries worked, I got excited about electrical power. I built a lighting-circuit. But after a short while, they dimmed. The batteries were going flat. Despair. But then I realised I could charge them from the alternator. They went.

After a fortnight, they went out again. This time the batteries were dry. They needed distilled water. I had salt water thundering round my shores. I had a brackish stream. I had volcanic geysers. But my island didn't have distilled water. From sections of the fuselage, I built a shallow basin. Then I made a tent of perspex over the top and filled the basin with water from the stream. As the sun got up, the water condensed on to the Perspex and ran down on the inside into a pair of collecting gutters. I syphoned it off and topped up my batteries with it. I had light again. Then after a couple of months it went out again.

One by one the bulbs fizzled out until I had none left. Even if I could develop glass-blowing (I had enough sand), I couldn't make a vacuum. My thoughts began to turn to other things. An electrical waste pump. But, one day, as I sat here, the thought struck me, What was I doing trying to produce energy to dispose of waste, when the waste itself was a source of energy.

I knew the principle, nothing could be simpler: waste matter, mixed to sludge with water, is added daily to a retainer-tank. Construct a valve. When this is opened, the in-put is gravity fed into the digester-tank. Every fresh addition to the retainer tank displaces an equivalent amount and causes it to overflow into the digester. The length of the digestion-process depends on the temperature of the digester-tank. After mounting some tests, I discovered that this varied between a fortnight and a month. The lower the temperature, the longer it took.

If retention-time took, say, ten days, then each day I would need, in order to keep the retainer-tank topped up, to provide one tenth of the total volume of waste in my system. If it took thirty-eight days, I would only need to add in one thirty-eighth. The gas then bubbles off the sludge and is syphoned off along a delivery-line to a gas holder. From there it enters the domestic system.

When I built my system, it was autumn. Retention time was about twenty-five days. I built a small primus and a gas lamp, making the mantle out of asbestos from part of the Piper's engine cowling. I found that my goats produced enough waste to power these two devices. I was excited. I extended my lighting system to my library and collected waste from some wild pigs to power this extension. Winter arrived. Temperatures sank. Retention time grew longer. Up to thirty and then thirty-seven days. Every day, I needed only a thirty-seventh of my total waste in order to power my modest collection of devices. All winter I worked, designing and building new devices to run off the system. I dreamt of mint juleps in the summer. I had the alcohol. I had the mint. All I needed was the gas-powered fridge to produce the ice. By the time the spring came, I had put many of these devices into operation, coping with the increased demand on my system by rounding up some wild pigs and penning them. I was so happy, I was starting to get bored.

I began designing a gas-powered rotary toothbrush and a gas-powered dune-buggy. Temperatures began to rise. At first I didn't notice. I felt no discomfort. I simply had to round up a few extra wild pigs, in order to cope with the fall in retention-time. I made more tanks to store their waste in. Gradually, the northern end of the island began to look like a cross between an oil refinery and a pig-sty. But it was all well away from my hutch.

Each day, the temperature rose a little and the retention time shrank. I rounded up all the wild pigs on the island and penned them. But I was down to ten days, and no sign of any let-up. I went out to their pens. It was beginning to worry me. I hadn't got the resources to feed them to produce enough waste. They looked ill. They could do no more. I'd come to the end of my resources. A debate started up.

Pro	Contra
It's necessary to cut the number of devices you are running off your system.	*No, this is only one conclusion . . .*
What do you really need? Do you, for example, really need a gas refrigerator?	*Yes . . .*
Such a large stove?	*Yes . . .*
Do you need the extra lighting for your library?	*Of course you do. How can you rewrite the bible from memory without proper lighting? The decency of your standard of living depends on the steady flow of excrement. You should be*

concentrating your powers on solving this technological question, not trying to reduce your standard of living . . .

It's a question of priorities . . . *The priority is to retain your standard of living . . .*

The priority is to survive . . . *What is the point of surviving in barbaric misery? String quartets do not get written when one squats all day in cold mud . . .*

Well well, to survive as happily as possible . . . *Happiness depends on a certain standard of living . . .*

Depends on how you define standard of living . . . *It is defined in terms of material comfort, and if your comfort slips one iota from its present level, it will cause you to be unhappy . . .*

You are a namby-pamby . . . *You may be that, but you'll be unhappy just the same and you know what you're like when you're unhappy . . .*

You're already unhappy at the thought of it, thus proving that unhappiness does not stem from an actual drop in your standard of living . . . *You are making yourself unhappy, it is not a necessary unhappiness, such as that caused by the lights going out . . .*

If you reduce the number of devices by one, you will be able to continue in medium unhappiness. Surely that is better than the alternative.

To continue a few days longer in a happiness you know to be illusory and then sink into absolute misery as your standard of living reduces absolutely. Besides, there's always the chance that in the

What alternative?

meantime you will solve the
technological problem. You
might find, for example, a
hidden cache of . . .

Compromises of this order are
shameful . . . No further
reductions after this one can be
tolerated . . .

Meanwhile temperatures went on rising. Retention time shrank
to five and then three days. I spent hours with buckets and a cart,
scouring the island for the slightest hint of a bird-dropping. I made
food-centres for the birds and collected their waste. I had thoughts
of breeding them, but the time at my disposal was shrinking. They
were too small to be really effective. I needed gannets, large birds.
But there was not a large bird in sight. In desperation I took away
my scarecrows. They came in large numbers and fed on my crops. I
got a certain amount more out of that. But soon they'd eaten all my
crops and, instead of dropping as I had anticipated, the temperature rose again in mid-June.

Retention-time was down to an incredible two days now. Every
day I had to produce a half of the waste. I'd now reached the point
where my own contributions were essential to the survival of the
system in its present form. Time was beginning to be a serious
problem. At first I was haphazard, running at top speed with the
cart from collection point to collection point and dashing back to
my seat. I had now connected this directly with the retainer tank by
bringing the valve in on a long line. By doing this I could open the
valve to let more in without leaving the seat. After a while I was
forced to do my collecting at night, because I had to spend all day
on the seat.

In the dead of night, I set out with my cart to collect the previous
day's load. By day, I took care to eat soft things in order to keep up
a perpetual state of diarrhoea. Gradually everything centred round
my seat, like the plates round a glutton. I moved the fridge in there,
so I could get the things out of it, to eat, to produce the waste, to
keep it going. In between times, I stuck a separate feedpipe into my

anus, in the hope of catching any stray clouds of gas that might be given off by my own processes of digestion. Weeping at the gripes in my belly, I spent all day producing the little extra that counted and all night trudging about the island with a torch collecting the rest. Inexorably, the temperature rose. Retention-time was now down to an unbelievable one day. But there were other problems to distract me by this time.

Once the methane had bubbled up through the sludge, I had to dump the waste. During the course of the summer, as temperatures rose and I needed more each day, I had dumped so much that the island now resembled a gigantic dung heap. I was restricted to carved avenues between black snowdrifts. The vegetation had begun to defoliate. My nightly collection journeys had become a blundering nightmare. In the dark, I found it difficult to tell sometimes which was fresh waste, and which was waste waste. Besides, I now had the added problem that I was forced to spend so much time on the seat that I could no longer afford to barrow the waste waste any distance.

I took to dumping it on the other side of the clearing. Then as the temperature crept up a couple of degrees, halfway across; then, finally, just outside the door.

Now the door wouldn't open any more. I was imprisoned. My lights and fridge were still working, but time was running out. I sat in the hot, steamy gloom, contemplating my store of mangoes in the fridge, and hesitating to switch on the gas lamp. It was dusk. The only light came from two small portholes high up in the wall. The stench was so powerful it made my ears crack. The stuff was oozing round the doorjamb. Outside I could imagine the island. Great undulating ranges of stale sludge, rippling in the wind like a rice pudding that was underdone and burnt at the same time.

I was on the point of destroying myself. I had to take action. Something was wrong somewhere. I was hunched in the dark like a troglodyte, toiling to produce comfort.

For whom? Not for me. For my alter ego, with his pretentious dream of culture and ease, who judged me to be born to sweat and groan in the dark. But he didn't have time to inhabit his dream. He saw himself as a poet, a musician, a noble castaway, leaning chin in hand over his study table, in a pool of light from a gently hissing lamp. The lamp hissed, but the library was empty. There was no alter ego. There was only me, despite the class difference between us. String quartets cannot be written while squatting in cold mud. The thought constipated me with anger. After a few minutes, I heard the gas pressure starting to fade. The pilot light went out in the water-heater. Water began to run under the fridge door. Finally, the light flickered, its hiss dying to a whisper, and went out. I took up my hammer and let in the stars. The surge of pleasure as I swung and swung at the tanks outside I can liken in its intensity only to a brief, honourable stool.

5   MY PARROT

I found my parrot lame in the forest and took him in and made a cage for him. That is not true. I did nothing of the kind. The truth is, I'm embarrassed by the fact that I don't remember how he came into my life. Sometimes I vary my little story. Sometimes it's he who takes the initiative. He flies on to my windowsill and sits there, his head cocked on one side as much as to say 'Buddy can you spare a dime.' Even though, in point of fact, he couldn't fly.

Neither was he a parrot. Neither was he a mynah, a greenfinch, nor a canary. He was a bird, indeed that much can be said, but a bird of such surpassing drabness that he had no name I could think of. To make things easier, I thought of him as my parrot. At first he was utterly silent. He watched me with dedication. One day, he produced a sound like a file rasping on a piece of sheet metal. For a long time, I pointedly ignored this parody of my breathing.

When I could endure it no longer, I brought home a mirror made from pieces of shell, which I put in his cage. He reverted to total silence, pecking it sulkily every now and again. I decided to take him in hand after this.

I taught him to whistle 'Lillibulero'. Then he went on to fragments of Handel, minuets, *bourrées*, *saltarellos* and the like. He could do an octave and a half. I was disappointed. On high Bs and Cs, I allowed him to be silent. Unfortunately he seemed to be built in C. I taught him everything I could remember – some of it in F major, which at first I had to transpose for him. Then when we had exhausted my simple stock, we tried variations. I'd hum a simple melody and he'd reply *maestoso*. I did a *scherzo*. He'd double up *poco piu mosso*. I'd riposte *poco meno mosso*. 'Twinkle Twinkle Little Star', I remember, went on for a week like this. After that we lost ourselves in the wilds of counterpoint, pausing only for food.

At first I was amused. Whole tracts of time were swallowed up in friendly competition. He now had complete chromatic control of himself and could perform in any key I liked. But he began to get obscure. He began to introduce baroque leaps and modulations I didn't understand and couldn't keep up with. It wasn't long before he'd passed completely out of my class. Gradually, he grew reluctant to play with me. When I approached the cage and made overtures, he looked down his beak at me. For months he indulged in a series of rhythmically obscure sonatas. One day I came in and found him doing a piece in canon with himself. After this I grew jealous of him.

His baroque period faded into rococo. His romantic period followed. Without knowing what I was doing, I had set him on a path. I was forced to watch, helpless, as he raved through his inevitable history. All I had to do was feed him. He perched alone in his cage hunched over his bits of maize like Beethoven at the piano. I gazed at him in awe. His voice in its richness and versatility resembled a church organ, whelming up and down in a series of wild fantasias and instant fugues.

His tiny beak opened and a vast inspiring hum came out of it, as if my living room were the organ-loft of a great cathedral. Or rather, when the beak opened, there was the sound a particularly loud record gives, a tense lull, sometimes with a faint rehearsal of the opening bars, before it begins. At this time my jealousy left me. I spent hours standing by his cage listening in a kind of trance. But soon he went into his modern period and this is when we really parted company. He started to produce twelve-tone chamber pieces that made me quite ill. He became obsessed by dissonance and then, after that, randomness. I baulked. That's not music, I said, that's *noise*. A child could do it. Our dialogue was over. All I could get out of him was an irregular sequence of muffled squeaks and whistles. My patience was exhausted. I begged with him. I pleaded. Why didn't he do some of those nice sarabandes? Or, if he liked, those Hungarian folk dance suites? For answer, I got something suspiciously like a burst of flatulence. I was angry. He would have to be taught a lesson.

I clapped a cloth over the cage one day, right in the middle of a very irritating piece for seven pianos and a washboard. Silence. Bravely, I whistled as I went about my business. Absolute quiet. I couldn't bear it. What was he doing? I didn't ask myself, What could he be doing? After all, the number of things a parrot (not to mention a pseudo-parrot) in a cage two foot by three, *could* be doing, is limited, to say the least. But not to me, whose relationship to him was that of sole living companion. Silence was a bad sign. I itched to whip off the cloth. Just lift up the corner. Was he dead? I posed the question to myself with a degree of detachment that did not deceive me. I was really interested in finding him at the bottom of the cage, his little feet in the air, his dear little eyes glassy. Each time I emptied his tray, putting my hand under the cloth to withdraw it, I had the idea that he would be lying in it.

He perceived my state of mind. Beneath the maroon-coloured cloth I had woven for this very purpose, he sensed my uncertainties. There were noises. At first he contented himself with simple imitations. My goats, for example. I went rushing out, thinking something was the matter with my nannies. But they were all asleep. Innocently, the cloth draped the cage. Silence. The numbers of things he could imitate in his immediate environment were limited indeed and he soon ran out of them. One day I heard distinctly through the open window the siren of a large ocean-going liner. I leapt up to the top of the hill, fumbling for my match to light my signal fire, the balm of its reverberations still in my ears. The cloth quivered.

Another time, I heard the slow drip of a tap somewhere. I looked suspiciously at the cage. But the dripping was overlaid with the tinkle of his little bell. I searched and found nothing, of course. When I came back, I could hear from beneath the cloth the derisive claque of crab-claws. I sat down. It began again, the slow drip with an interval between each sound that seemed almost intolerably long. His timing was perfect. But he was bored, I could tell. I was determined not to take off the cloth.

As he realised this, the intensity and range of his ventriloquism increased. Some days he had me down in the corner, my hands over my ears, trying to shut out the hideous coughing, the radio switched rapidly from station to station. He got more ambitious, homing in on the most intimate memories of my childhood. The sound of my brother beneath the sheets on a winter's evening, toiling, purple-faced with duty, at his pleasure. The shout of the rag-and-bone man, and the simultaneous accompaniment of his hand bell, as he paused outside the house on Saturday mornings. Still, I resisted. Then finally, the sound of Bristol, my aunt's tomcat. This act of hubris was almost his undoing. At first, he was content with conventional miaowing. I paid no attention. It was hard, but I did it. But then he succeeded in making the curious noise that Bristol made when he was aware of a bird. A kind of strangled croak, a creak, outrageously pathetic, quite different from all the other sounds he made, as if he were praying for this fluttering flying thing to land in front of him and give him a chance. Take pity, creaked Bristol, Take pity on a poor, wingless Pussy . . . This was a dangerous game for a bird to play. With any luck he might overstep the mark and catch himself. The growling, interspersed with cunning cheeps, increased until there was a sudden flurry of activity, astonishingly authentic noises of scratching and biting and then the scrunch of small bones.

I couldn't stand it any longer. I knew I should not find him crushed but still breathing on the floor of his cage. But there was a chance that he'd given his gallant little heart a thundering attack from the efforts of imitation. I rushed to the cage and whipped off the cloth. He sat swinging serenely back and forth. I had begun by regarding him as the emblem of my state. An island unto himself. In his cage, he seemed a castaway, a creature totally alone, unaware of everything outside himself. From that he had turned to the opposite extreme, a creature so aware of me that by sheer empathy he could produce the sound of the 'Hinton Manor' slipping on a frosty track at Mile Bank at 12.05 on January 18th, 1947. I couldn't bear it any longer. I opened the door of the cage. Go on, I shouted, You're free, you horrible bird.

He crouched at the entrance to the cage, not moving. He was emaciated. It's difficult for a parrot to be emaciated, but he achieved it at that moment. I looked at him. He looked back at me, his dull eye cocked. It was then that I saw him differently. For the first time, I saw him as he really was. Perhaps in that moment, he had a certain awareness of how I saw him. The eye that looked at me boasted its autonomy, but beneath its eyelids bored a mass of roundworms; the feathers of his sleek chest were tenements, bursting with generations of flies and lice; beneath them, crawling and digging into the surface of the skin, roamed a mass of ticks; in the holes in his beak, jammed like city pedestrians in a subway, struggled crowds of mites, roundworm and fungi; in the intestines, the tapeworm lengthened blindly in its warm bath of half-digested food; in the bloodstream sailed an armada of viruses; in the brain that conducted whatever electro-chemical messages of alertness to me he could muster, tiny cataracts of protozoans and bacteria spilled from one level to another . . . all of them burrowing, moving, pressing through the walls of tissue as if they were not there, as if *he* were not there, from the heart to the lungs, from the lungs to the windpipe, from the windpipe to the gullet, from the gullet to the alimentary tract, from the alimentary tract to the intestines, through the walls of the intestines into the bloodstream, inexorably sweeping round into the heart, from the heart to the lungs . . .

He remained, crouching at the entrance to the cage door, traumatised perhaps by my vision of him. After a moment, I closed the cage and took it out to the stream, where I lowered it into the water and left it hanging there on a piece of string. When I raised it up in the evening, the cage was occupied by a fish, so fat it had become jammed against the bars. It looked at me with its cold eye, its mouth open like an opera singer's. I took it home, still jammed in the cage, and waited patiently for it to expire. Nothing happened. Time went on. I thought of the struggles of the bacteria-within-the-bird-within-the-fish. Even now they were sweeping the backbone of this new environment, much like the old, threading their way in vast, jostling armies through the wet tissues, each carrying within itself another system of cellular struggle, great herds of micro-organisms grazing the plains of its tiny body.

The fish sat and stared back. It wasn't going to work. I daren't leave it any longer. It was beginning to disturb my equilibrium. Besides, I had begun to detect, faintly issuing from that open pout, the sound of a Puccini aria. I grew nervous. I went back to the stream to drown the fish. It wasn't the fish I was drowning, of course, but the bird, the bird-within-the-fish. I held it under. It wriggled. From the open mouth came a series of bubbles which broke on the surface: I heard the sound, as I felt it slipping about in my hands, of distant news vendors on a city street and then, faint but true, the noise of a door opening and shutting, sometimes slamming, sometimes being shut politely, sometimes being hammered on by a reluctant occupant. It was too much. Letting it go could be very dangerous. I'd risk having a musical river running by my back door. Or worse, a river that could throw its voice.

I took the fish home, got out my frying pan, and cast him struggling into a pool of smoking goat's fat. His backbone curled dutifully, his eyes whitened, his tail struggled up into a slow lash, then settled, sticking to the pan. I threw more logs on the fire, then held the pan by means of rags and then, when it was red hot, a long pole I use for retrieving the loaves from my oven when they are done. It charred. Then leaped and flamed for a moment. My curiosity overcame me. I took it out. The moment of folly. An ash-like disk, the size of a shilling, remained in the centre of the blackened pan. My resolve, was it the weakening of it? I shall never know. All I know is that, as I poked in this piece of ash, I heard it whispering.

And the next day, as I winnowed it from the cliff, I heard the sound of a scimitar descending within centimetres of my ear, a sound which modulated into the hum of Gregory Peck's cane vanishing out of his hand in a celluloid Alpine drama I couldn't remember the name of.

6 GETTING BACK

Why not just lie under a palm, like the old sailor, and wait to be rescued? Forget about this nonsense. Oblivion is reluctant to respond to my hoarse maydays, one must think of the economics of rescue I suppose. But waiting for inanition to do its work is like waiting for the earth to cool, or the friendly sun to move away into the darkness: it would be interesting, but one just hasn't the time. To spice it a little, I stake myself out for the ants. One arm is free, it's a problem for the ants, whose sense of credibility tends to be too sharp for comfort, but do they really care about such details? Surely I can rig something up? I can use my free hand to wave to them. They pay not the slightest attention. They march on by, their dressing impeccable, eyes to the front, carving their swath a quarter of an inch from my outstretched arm. Strains of 'It's a long, long way to Tipperary' float from their disappearing column. Furious, I get up and manacle myself to the inside of a safe. Safes don't exactly lie around on palm-strewn beaches, but I've made it of wood, even squashing sea-snails over it for the silvering. I roll myself laboriously, corner to corner, down to the shallows, deeper and deeper until I'm not visible from the shore any longer, only to rise in thirty seconds, holding my chains aloft in a triumph of reluctance. It's no good. The light blinds, and the panic rises again.

Not this time, Mother, I shout, remembering Houdini, just one more show and then we can be together . . . All I want, apparently, is to stifle, roast, drown, concuss, bleed my way through one of nature's thousand yawning exits. Apparently. But when my mind, locked up in its tower of rotting meat, lets down like Rapunzel its golden S.O.S. into the ether, where is my Prince? Anxiously, I cup my ear and, growing louder, I hear them at last, the clack of coconut shells and the jingle of his fake bridle. I rush from window to window. Nothing. Instead, a massed choir of schoolboys is emerging from the woods and gathering to stand in the ornamental rockeries and flowerbeds at the foot of the tower. They strike up

New every morning is the love
Awakening and uprising prove

and in the front row, I recognise myself, cap over my large ears, socks rolled down, foremost among the trebles.

I'm being managed. I'm being run by a dinner table, well beyond the threshold of my perception, around which a few bloated figures of both sexes let roll about their mouths a liquid so golden and subtle, it can only be apprehended as liquid through a lifetime's apprenticeship of drinking similar liquids, served by androgynous blondes, whole choruses of them, lying back on scarlet tapestries plucking indolently at stringed instruments, whose sounds tremble through the air with a sweetness so thrilling it's like a shock of cold water.

Occasionally, into one of the intervals between lolling eating serving playing drinking rolling new things round the palate, falls a fat bloodshot remark, a blurred saying, squeezed through the red graph-paper of broken capillaries, through lips whose epithelial tissue has withered into leather from the fine things that have passed them. Both ways. The sweetmeats that have gone in, and the wisdom that has flowed out. Dribbling, in its generosity, in its anxiety to set me to rights, out of the nostrils. Smacking of purity for me. Smacking of lips for me. A place for me to start from, a germless saw.

Property is a theft, and I cannot return my body to its owner. There's no place to begin my journey from. Back, back, seeking to get up the anus of my father, back into his intestines where it really matters. Back, back. Getting at my mother's red truth by unzipping her labia all the way up to the chin. Before my brothers do it first. It's no good. All the time, the bacteria are there, thriving in the plasma of the ideal. In their hordes they scurry, sweeping over the steppes of the idea like the extras in a Russian epic. The sky here is so full of unidentified flying objects, wing tip to wing tip, nose to tail, that it might be just the sky. I can't see my hand before my face here. Not that I need to. There are no Venetian plots, no daggers in the hand, no death, no coups, no applause while the catharsis bubbles in the brain like caustic soda, not even a fatal auto on the street after the theatre.

I put my hands over my ears. It's the opening of the exhibition. It's a sequence of drawings. The first shows a company of people sipping their drinks in a well appointed drawing-room, busily chatting about horse-racing, or the latest on the stock-market. I'm in there somewhere, but you can't quite see me. Just behind the third person on the right's shoulder. The next has narrowed to a few friends, all of whom agree with one another about everything. They do nothing but agree, nursing their differences of opinion by agreeing. I'm in there too, somewhere, my head nodding like a puppet, but you can't see me. Then I'm alone with a woman in the next one. You'd think you could see me now, but the angle shows her head and shoulders from the back and another body you can't quite make out. Then in the next I'm alone. You'd think you could see me there. Sitting in my chair in the middle of the room. But the chair's a high-winged armchair, such as are used to good effect in B movies, and only one of my arms is visible. In the next, the chair has gone and you'd think you could see me now, fallen perhaps in a heap on the floor, naked, my prick tumbling about on my lap, rather bad pencilling at that point perhaps. But the room is empty, except for my signature in the corner on one of the chequered tiles.

7   UNCREATIVE THINKING

Banalities, column after column, generation after generation, refugees from some collapsed regime of the commonplace, come tramping over the borders of my mind. I stand, watching them go by: a local farmer whose initial outrage has given way to resignation; and who dreams, just occasionally, of a celestial ghetto they could all file into, the last one looking round in a sensitive fashion before closing, softly, carefully and for ever, the door. I don't want them here. But they seem inevitable.

I've tried the liberal approach. Recognising them, giving them democratic rights. Making each and every futile pleonasm responsible for itself, giving it a good standard of living, encouraging holy matrimony and the right to give birth to others. An analogy, of course. They can't have ideas, I am fully aware of that, they are naive, they can't *think*. They'd be free if only they could realise it.

As it is, they're open to any direction, any persuasion. Coming or going, it's all one to them. They can't *do* anything, except bustle away at being what they are like stationary Buddhists. I'm always taking them in, or rather, being taken in by them. Because they aren't free, they persuade me that I'm not. That I must house them, listen to their lives, their tabloid necessities. They waddle up to me, transparent, but somehow elephantine, pushing in front of them the bloated bellies of which they're so proud. Or sometimes, with a vanity which in other circumstances would be touching, they try to conceal from me the fact that once again they're gravid with cliché. Then I'm made to feel sluggish, my thoughts wearing clothes that no longer fit, pear-shaped thoughts.

What I need to do is go in for a spot of uncreative thinking. It ought to be possible, with a little effort, a little concentration, to run these tautologies out of my mind like drunks out of a closing bar.

Let us call him Arthur. And her? Pearl.

They don't know that I am going to get rid of them.

They are sitting down on the sofa. Arthur has come home early because he's felt queasy all day at work. Pearl feels queasy too. Earlier in the day, she's rung Arthur up to tell him so, thus annoying his employer, because they have a rule at the Gas Show-rooms that personal calls to the sales assistants during working hours are not allowed. They think it's something they've eaten. The packet paella that Pearl made the night before. If they could think about it, they would date it from that moment on.

At first, their friends can't believe how young they're looking. Everyone remarks on it, some with malice. Arthur, now in his mid-thirties and beginning to thicken round the middle, loses with every day that passes his stolid look. He walks with a springier step. He thinks again of Honey, the chorus girl he met one night under Vauxhall Bridge after the annual Gas Conference. Pearl too is beginning to look much livelier, and hardly seems pregnant at all. It even appears as if Arthur is getting some of his hair back. Everybody notices it. They are happy. But then it starts getting a bit inconvenient.

At first it's only the minor inconvenience of forgetting the future and remembering the past. Arguments, as between any happily married couple, break out between them from time to time. But they are invariably centred about some past event.

They go to the *Châlet Suisse* one night for their dinner and have a difference of opinion about which hotel they stayed in on the Costa Brava on their last holiday four years earlier. Arthur, as usual, insists that he is right. I can remember it, as if it were yesterday, he says reassuringly. The next morning they wake up sunburnt. They can't understand it. It's very embarrassing to both of them, because they're almost black, but they haven't been anywhere. All their friends will ask, Where have you been? We don't know.

Arthur takes a week off work, just to make it a bit more credible. So they stay at home, worrying about their suntan and the memories of sunlight and crowded beaches and stinking drains and cheap cognac which – thrust them back as they may – are flooding their minds.

By Thursday, Arthur can't stand it any more and decides to go down to the pub for a lunchtime drink. See his mates, bluff it out. He goes out to his Cortina and gets in. The floor is sandy. He ignores it and starts up the engine. But he sits there in the garage with the engine running, because a horrible thought has just entered his mind. Supposing the boot is full of suitcases. He gets out and, hardly daring to look, opens it. They still have their Lunn-Poly labels on. Pearl is crying, because she knows already what he has found.

She's been thinking about it, you see. At first she was pleased that some of the clothes she had before she got pregnant still fitted. But now she's worried. She goes to the doctor because she's losing so much weight. Her interview with the doctor is very confusing. He begins by talking to her about the post-natal clinic, while he tests her blood pressure. Pearl breaks into tears and says she feels funny. Been for a holiday, he says brightly as she undresses. Lovely sun tan. But his face clouds as he feels her belly.

He takes off his glasses. Where did you go? he asks.

It's my infra-red, says Pearl.

I *meant*, to have this done, he gestures at her belly.

Nowhere, says Pearl. What d'you mean?

Well, says the doctor, if that's your attitude . . . He takes off his glasses and bursts into a speech. He tells her that kind of thing is immoral – we both know what we're talking about – it's tantamount to murder. It is a kind of murder, in fact. In fact, she is a kind of murderer.

Pearl bursts into tears again. But I didn't . . . *I didn't* . . .

Mrs Rutter, says the doctor, there is no point in lying about it. I can understand your concealing the address from me, but to lie about it having happened is just plain stupidity.

I don't know what happened, wails Pearl to the firmly closing door, I don't know . . . I've just *lost* it . . .

What are they going to tell their parents? In the end, they have to pretend to have had it aborted. They become objects of pity. Pearl can't have any more children. Now it's Arthur's turn to have problems. He finds he's beginning to behave rather strangely at work. The encyclopaedic knowledge he has of the customers' accounts seems to be vanishing from his head. His files are depleted. He asks Raymond, an unheard of thing. He knows Raymond doesn't have a clue. He's helpless. He even asks Carol. Carol gets annoyed, because Arthur was there in the office long before she arrived. Even before Raymond arrived.

One day soon afterwards Arthur and Pearl are having lunch in their kitchen when who do they see through the picture-window coming up the drive but Arthur's boss Mr Mellors. He's very friendly. He's come to give Arthur a lift. No, he won't come in. But he's pleased to meet Pearl. On the way out, he insists on going into the garage and getting out Arthur's bicycle, a rusty old thing. He wheels it out to his car and ties it elaborately to the back of the open boot. Arthur is still pondering about why Mr Mellors has insisted on introducing himself to Pearl as if he's never met her. On the way to work, Mr Mellors is hearty, laughing and making jokes all the time about Arthur's future. They even stop at a pub for a drink.

When they eventually get to work, Mr Mellors asks him to sit down on a chair outside his office and wait. After twenty minutes, he comes out, his face flushed and says, as if he doesn't know him, Mr Rutter? Arthur gets up and follows him into the office. Behind the desk are seated three other men. The air is thick with cigarette smoke. Mr Mellors introduces Arthur to the other men and asks him politely to take a seat. With a sigh that sounds a bit artificial to Arthur, Mr Mellor sits down himself.

Good God, thinks Arthur, it's a promotion committee.

Mr Mellors beams. Well, Gentlemen, is there anything you want to add, he asks. The other men all shake their heads and murmur. Then I think I can safely say, Mr Rutter, in *front* of you, that your application has been successful . . . Arthur is puzzled. As far as he knows he hasn't applied for promotion. But visions of a new car, possibly even a new house, are beginning to spring up. These are interrupted by an abrupt change of expression on Mr Mellors' face. He seems almost hostile as he goes on to ask Arthur a pointed question about his attitude towards withdrawal of labour in the event of a dispute with the management. This is rather unexpected.

Arthur stammers out his non-committal answer, but before he can finish it, the man on his left raps out another question about baths filling from one another. The man on his left changes it to a sum about approaching railway trains. Arthur is getting really nervous now. The questions are piling in thick and fast. Arthur is beginning to wonder how much longer he can hold out, he's quaking that much with fear and anxiety, when Mr Mellors opens a drawer in his desk and pushes a folder into it. Then they all smile at Arthur, as if this is some kind of recondite signal, and Mr Mellors asks Arthur if he's had a good trip and welcomes him to the office. Then they all stand and shake hands with him one by one.

Mr Mellors takes Arthur out, through the main office, past the typists, into the street, where he shows Arthur how to get his bicycle out of the rack. He holds it while Arthur mounts, making a series of jokes about previous experience and aptitude which strike Arthur, under the circumstances, as being downright sadistic. Disconsolate and rigid with nervous tension, he rides home to Pearl. In an appalled, half-believing way, he tells her the news. But Pearl astonishes him by dragging him upstairs and trying to make love to him.

Doesn't she realise that he's just lost his *job*, under mysterious circumstances? Pearl doesn't care. She's silly. She puts on her shorty nightie and pours him a whisky.

After an hour or so, Arthur doesn't care either.

What if he has been there three years? He can always get another job. Pearl looks good in her nightdress. They've got a bit in the bank.

They start getting up late, sometimes even after the pubs have shut. Making love enthusiastically until they're weak at the knees. Even waking up in the middle of the night and leaping on each other. Arthur starts telling Pearl how much he loves her. She loves him too. The house looks strangely empty, because, she reveals, she's sold one or two articles of furniture. All the more for booze, jokes Arthur.

They spend a week in Blackpool, dancing and fucking and going to shows and clasping each other in high winds down the golden mile.

When they get back, Arthur takes Pearl, wearing her best pink costume with lemon accessories, to the Registry Office. The photographer is waiting outside. Arthur's mother and Pearl's father are weeping. They burst in through a cloud of confetti. There's a short ceremony, after which Arthur and Bilko his best man, rush down the steps with the ring they've just drunkenly pulled off Pearl's finger, into Bilko's waiting car and drive off. After an anxious period of waiting, everyone leaves in separate cars.

The next day Arthur goes to Pearl's house and starts taking her out. At first they don't bother to go out very often. Much better to wait for Pearl's mother to go to bingo and then slip into her bed. But then, as time goes on, her mother stays in too. She even stays up after the television's finished, when Arthur's desperate to have Pearl on the rug in front of the fire. But this he doesn't seem to be able to manage any more, because Pearl's become unaccountably shy. What on earth is the matter with her? It's not as if they haven't done it before. Things are getting more and more distant. It almost seems to Arthur as if she doesn't want to see him. She's avoiding him.

Then he hears from one of his friends that Pearl has another boyfriend. One day Arthur sees them together. He's found out about the dance in the Church Hall. Drunk, he turns up on his motorbike. He goes into the dance and knocks down Pearl's boyfriend. Pearl picks him up and they leave together. After that, Pearl won't have anything to do with Arthur. He has a last glimpse of her, looking in a shoe-shop window. Then he sees her no more. Pearl quarrels with her new boyfriend and, shortly after, stops having periods.

Arthur sells his BSA and buys a bike. He starts going to school. For a couple of years, he rides it up the school drive every morning. Then he falls off it, one Saturday afternoon, and never gets on again. He takes it to the shop and sells it to the man and goes home and gives his father the money.

His father puts it in a pot on the mantelpiece. Arthur immediately goes into a ranting, screaming fit, yelling at the top of his voice that he wants his bicycle. He rushes out into the garden and accidentally sticks a fork through his leg. We smile at these accidents. Such is the legacy of having had a bicycle.

Meanwhile Pearl acquires the habit of playing with dolls. She and Cedric from next door go up to the bathroom and strip their clothes off. He shows her his cock. She's intrigued. She shows him her cunt, with the hairs beginning to show. He pokes at it with his blackberry-stained finger. They pee in each other's mouths. Pearl is destined never to see another cock, except her father's, one day, as he stands by the bedroom door with it hanging out of his underpants.

Arthur has shat himself in school and runs home through the town, fleeing from the playground with the yellow runny shit caked on his shirt-tails, a puzzled feeling inside his head. It's his last day. He's doomed never to go again. He begins to shit himself regularly, so much so that his mother puts him in special little padded trousers that absorb the shit and prevent it from running down his legs and smelling so much. Frustrated, Arthur starts wetting the bed and not getting up. When he does get up, he staggers like a drunk and falls down. He almost knocks his eye out on the corner of the sideboard. His teeth have disappeared, shrinking down into his gums. He looks like a diminutive old man. He gets more teeth, but they're not so good and come out easily. No more come after they've all gone.

Pearl's sexual organs wither, the hairs fall out, the breasts tighten up into little knots and her mother notices one day that they've vanished into two pink dents in her pigeon-chest. She too eventually succumbs to incontinence and leaves school. Eventually, after a lot of trouble at the dentists and crying at night, she's left with one tiny stump pushing up out of her gum. One day her father persuades her, for a game, to tie it to a piece of cotton. He tells her he's going to show her a trick. He goes over to the door, winding out the cotton. Pearl can feel the thread almost cutting her lips. He ties it to the doorknob and tells her to stand still. Then he goes through the door, slamming it after him. Bewildered Pearl looks at her last bloody stump on the floor. That night, when she goes upstairs and feels under her pillow for her sixpence, she finds the fairies have put her stump there instead.

And Arthur is forgetting how to talk. His language begins audibly to decay. His parents are worried. At first, he launches bravely on sentences which he can't finish. But then he can't start them either. Desperately, each day, he loses a word or a phrase, until he's reduced to gurgling and banging his spoon. His parents begin to feed him from their plates. After that, giving up in despair when he can't manage it, they mix him his own special soft food. His own apricot sauce, out of tins and jars. He's not allowed to sit by them any more, but has to be strapped into a high chair. He eats only a porridge of milk and rusks, which when left hardens to the consistency of set glue. He sits banging his spoon and throwing this mixture about the room until the furniture is caked in it. The Allied bombers drone over the house. Pearl starts wetting the bed.

A little later, after both of them are confined to their beds, Hitler emerges from his bunker with Eva Braun and a few friends and takes his first whiff of the world that is soon to be his. Then one night in the midst of the blitz Arthur wakes his mother. She takes him in her arms. He's wailing and sobbing. Arthur's father rings for the District Nurse.

In the nick of time, the nurse arrives and he helps her tip his son upside down and get labour started. He stands holding a bowl of hot water, not knowing what to do, as the hefty red-faced nurse shouts PULL NOW and REST NOW and his son's cries grow fainter and fainter, until they are stifled altogether and his tiny feet alone are visible. These damn breeches are always a problem, says the nurse. Soon the aperture has contracted to the size of a shilling. The nurse packs her bag and leaves.

For Pearl too, the time has come. It's a sunny day as, wrapped in a shawl, she's carried out to the ambulance in her mother's arms. Her mother is pale and exhausted, but happy. Her father sits with them as they drive to the hospital. They smile at Pearl, alas, and take her tiny fingers in their hands. They are so happy. Soon the ambulance arrives and is greeted by a bevy of waving nurses. One of them takes Pearl. Another supports Pearl's mother up the seven flights of stairs to the labour ward. Pearl's father is not allowed beyond the door. He must wait now for two long weeks. Happily, Pearl's mother settles into the ward. Pearl has finally lost her name. She lies, eyes closed, sucking listlessly from her mother's teat, as if she were aware of what's going to happen. After a week, she's smaller and weaker and her mother begins to feel weak too. The nurses pay them special attention. There's talk of an oxygen tent for the baby. She's eventually taken from her mother, who lies too ill even to notice. The father waits desperately at home. A day or so later, the tiny baby and the desperately weak mother are wheeled into the operating theatre. The father has arrived and waits downstairs. After eighteen hours of pacing, a nurse appears to tell him that everything is all right. He can take his wife home. She is immensely swollen and in great pain. He orders a taxi. He holds her hand in great concern. When they get home, they go to bed and fall asleep. Next morning the pain is hardly there. Pearl is a thing of the past. Soon she's only desperately wanted. Soon after that she's only a thought in the back of their minds, a general idea . . .

In this way, whole novels of the Russian variety could be written, vast researches undertaken to track down and extinguish the origins of Pearl and Arthur's trees. Pointless. I shall never arrive. Doubly pointless, because it's not necessary any more. As I look up, weighing this body of mine on the balls of my feet, my mind's full of the angle of the sun and nothing else.

◼━◀ CHATTO FICTION ▶━◼

Chatto Fiction presents adventurous writing at a reasonable price. Each month we publish exciting new fiction from all over the world in simultaneous hardback and paperback editions.

If you would like to know about the list and forthcoming titles, write to us at: 40 William IV Street, London WC2N 4DF.

Antonio Lobo Antunes
South of Nowhere

Manlio Argueta
One Day of Life

Maggie Brooks
Loose Connections

Sergei Dovlatov
The Compromise

Rikki Ducornet
The Stain

M. F. K. Fisher
Not Now But Now

Barbara Hanrahan
Kewpie Doll

Jorge Ibargüengoitia
The Dead Girls

Mary Keene
Mrs Donald

Jessie Kesson
Another Time, Another Place

Manuel Mujica Lainez
The Wandering Unicorn

Anne Leaton
*Good Friends, Just
Mayakovsky, My Love*

Bobbie Ann Mason
Shiloh and Other Stories

M. S. Power
Hunt for the Autumn Clowns

Emily Prager
A Visit from the Footbinder

Joseph Roth
*The Emperor's Tomb
Job: the Story of a Simple Man*

Josef Skvorecky
The Swell Season

Elizabeth Tallent
In Constant Flight

James Thackara
America's Children

Snoo Wilson
Spaceache

SHILOH
Bobbie Ann Mason

Bobbie Ann Mason writes with sympathy and pinpoint accuracy about small-town Kentucky lives in a time of change. Her stories represent some of the most exciting writing in America today, and they are a delight to read; poignant, funny and utterly universal in their appeal. *Shiloh*, her first collection, was nominated for the National Book Critics Circle Award, the American Book Awards, and the PEN/Faulkner Award, and was greeted with rare acclaim:

'A quite exceptional debut . . . Her characters are vivid presences, brought to fictional life with a hard-earned effortlessness, in prose that seems as natural as breathing' – *Observer*

'Her stories' flawless observation, their poet's concentration of language, their infallible sense of rhythm, of proportion, of balance, assault the reader with an unbroken shock wave of pleasure' – *New Statesman*

'Miss Mason's talent and craftsmanship are formidable. *Shiloh* shows not only how good she can be but how consistently good she remains. The most improbable thing about this volume is that not a single page lags, hardly a paragraph fails, not one among the 16 stories is less than impressive' – *New York Times*